# Daughters
# of
# Donegal

ISBN: 979-8-834822-81-3

First Edition: July 2022

Cover by SHG Design, AZ, USA

The triqueta (or triquetra) three-cornered symbol on the cover is a common design seen in many archaeological sites around Europe and into Anatolia dating from centuries BC. In early Celtic design, it has been used as a depiction of the triple goddesses: The Maiden, the Mother and the Crone. In later Christian times, it has been labelled the Trinity knot.

# Daughters
# of
# Donegal

## Evelyn Blaine Durkin

Mary Meehan Blaine with daughters Myra (left) and author Evelyn. In this May 1932 passport photo, Mary is pregnant with Patrick George. The immigration stamp recorded the group's re-entry into the US in May 1933.

# I

The pearly dimness of the passing summer night was dissolving in the light of the sun as it broke over the eastern hills. As Ellen watched from the open Dutch half-door of the house, she could see silhouetted against the brightness a drover urging his flock to market. It was time to be leaving. Her baskets of bread and the handiwork she had to sell were packed in the cart. Her father would soon be ready. She would wait in the cart.

As she crossed the yard, some of the young men idling by the gate started to banter with her. Because she was young and pretty, because they were young and admiring, because it was summer, she stopped to chat and maybe flirt a bit.

Immediately by the change in their faces she knew that her father, Peter McGuinness, or one of her brothers had come from the house. She turned and climbed into the cart just ahead of her father.

Oh well, there it was in a nutshell. She would be twenty soon, and her father had rejected every offer. Her mother Mary had died in 1880, just three years before. Since then Ellen had taken on the management of the home farm, and all the household, for her father and six brothers.

She knew they loved her, but it was a love nurtured by

convenience and custom. Her father in his grief would not release her, and her brothers reveled in the freedom from any domestic responsibilities. While she remained to care for them, they were under no pressure to change. She ruled in the house; they did not cross her, but she was not able to temper their behavior. Outside of her domain they worked and played together and were the scourge of the county. Eventually the oldest son would marry because, as was the custom, he would inherit everything his father held. Then the others would scatter like wild geese to America, Australia, Canada, wherever they could prosper.

Her father, who doted on them, could not, would not allow this, so he held her hostage and encouraged every wild venture the brothers could think of in his desire to keep them near. In the confusion of his grief and selfishness, he was not concerned with her needs and wishes.

The future stretched before her. It might be ten or more years before her eldest brother settled, and then the house would not be hers. The new wife would be mistress, and Ellen's chances of making a good match would have disappeared.

Nevertheless, the day was bright and clear, a rare day for the north of Ireland; she would enjoy what she could. Along with her friend Catherine Conwell she had a good booth at the fair and they would do a brisk business selling tea, fresh breads and cake. She also had her winter's embroidery to sell, and since it was much in demand by the English women, wives to the officers at the barracks, there would be a good profit at the end of the day. For now, however, she had only to sit and enjoy the warm sun and the smell of the salt on the westerly breeze blowing in from the Atlantic.

The horse trotted along. Friends and neighbors waved and hallooed as they passed.

§§§

George Meehan stood staring into the west at the puddled darkness of the sea in the shadow of the hills. He had sat late into the night with Canon Sweeney and got little enough sleep after he arrived home. In the brilliance of the early morning sun, he was examining the decision he had made the night before.

He felt a fool and yet could not bring himself to abandon the plans he and the canon had made. God knows, he should have married years ago. But he treasured the life he led. With no kith nor kin to question him and in possession of a large, profitable plantation, he bought every book and newspaper available and had long quiet nights to read or sit with his friends discussing the condition of the world – sure it was enough to keep any wise man occupied.

When he was in need of more society he knew he was welcome at any fireside. Much sought after for his advice and learning, he was also aware that he was still considered a most eligible catch. But over the years he had become adept at avoiding any serious relationship. He had done his share of courting but had never met the girl or woman who could hold his fancy. Until now. Well, every man had his Waterloo, and his had come to him.

Although he had attended the wake when Ellen McGuinness's mother died, he had paid little attention then to the young daughter ravaged with grief and surrounded by the keening women. He was not well acquainted with the family but knew them to be hard-working and prosperous.

3

Nevertheless, he saw little in their lifestyle to recommend them. It was well known that the McGuinness lads were as mad as hares.

But over the past year or so, he had become increasingly aware of Ellen's presence at all the céilís, hooleys, wakes, weddings and religious occasions which were the heart of the village social life in their village of Killybegs.

At first his was a disinterested study of how she would cope with the wild heedless bunch whom her mother had barely held in check. Despite all the calamitous predictions and to the secret consternation of the doomsayers, Ellen managed to hold her own, and as he watched something caught his heart.

The word he used to himself was gallant. She never relaxed her splendid carriage, nor did she encourage the town gossips who commiserated in hopes of becoming her confidant. Her troubles were her own, and deal with them she would. Nevertheless, there was no hope that her situation would improve given her father's refusal to entertain any offer for her hand and her brothers' careless indifference to her welfare.

George was aware that when she attended a dance, usually with her friend Catherine, she danced every jig, reel or round dance – but never more than twice with any young lad. It was known that if she encouraged any one of them, one or more of her brothers would appear at her side. The offender was usually a young man from another village, unaware of the situation. Ellen knew from experience that he would be subject to jostling, elbowing and baiting until he left or one of the older men intervened. It had not yet ended in serious injury, but this was undoubtedly due solely to the fact that the young men of Killybegs were not anxious to take on six hostile brothers, and visitors did not want trouble outside of their own place. Knowing this, she was careful to show no interest in any one lad, and there was tacit consent among the people in the village to do their best to protect her and, incidentally, any innocent visitors. George Meehan admired her for her steady good humor and dignity.

So there it was. She was lovely, it was true, but he had many a fine woman eager to make herself available. At his age, over twenty years older than the girl, he simply wanted to keep and protect her.

He had no answer for his desire and had resigned himself to the futility of it all. On the prior night, however, mellow with good whiskey, fine tobacco and the knowledge that he would be seeing her at the fair, he revealed his dilemma to Canon Sweeney. After his admission he regretted having opened his thoughts to another. It was not like him, nor did he want to be taken for an old fool yearning after a green girl.

To his everlasting surprise, the canon sat erect in his chair and almost shouted, "Why man dear, that's the solution."

As George Meehan sat staring, the canon explained himself. He had, he said, been worrying at the situation for a year or so. It was well known that the girl had been the object of many young men's desires, and that the father refused to even consider any offer. And although the canon at first had sympathized with Peter McGuinness, knowing the man to be devastated by the death of his wife, he was increasingly aware that something had to be done. It was unfair to the girl. And in view of the hostility of her father and brothers to any advances, the parents of young, eligible men were advising their sons that they wanted to hear "no nonsense" about Ellen McGuinness. Life was hard enough without calling down the wrath of that mad bunch.

In addition, the canon was of the opinion that "there would be bloodshed without a doubt" if the brothers were allowed to continue their intemperate behavior. Already there had been mutterings among the men, married and single alike, concerning lures sent out from the mad bunch to the village's wives, daughters and sweethearts. The six brothers were not unaware of their raw appeal.

"Do you not see, George," the canon sputtered. "Although I have spoken to the father time and time again, it has been a waste. The man is obdurate and knows well I cannot force a match where the parents of any interested young man are fearful.

"But he would have no lever with you. You have no relations who would be vulnerable. You've got the respect of every person in Killybegs, and enough holdings to be the envy of many. I know your concern over the age issue, and I understand your reluctance. But only think what her life will be like in a few years, given her brothers' history. Do you think the eldest son will even see or much care if any woman he marries treats Ellen as a servant? I hold no great hope that he will pick a woman sensitive enough to be kind.

"But without Ellen to fetch and carry for them, the other brothers will do what they should have done long ago: Seek their own fortunes and leave the village – and I might add myself – in peace.

"And don't forget the other consideration, which some of the men in the village have already raised with you: If you die without an heir – and there is no person who qualifies – the land will revert to the crown, and God knows they will grab it quickly enough. No man in Killybegs will sleep well at night knowing that every move could be observed from the hill in back of your house."

The two men sat quietly for awhile, Meehan deep in thought and the canon content to let George pursue the possibilities and consequences of the matter. Presently the canon chuckled and asked:

"Do you mind, George, the day those hellions took Roger Cunningham's cart? He could not discover where it had gone until a party of English walkers asked, in the public house, 'Why is there a cart floating on pig bladders in the loch?' The English were sure they had stumbled on some arcane ritual. And I was sure there would be murder done that day — Roger was that angry.

"It was a very near thing, but sure not one of those scamps had the grace to apologize. And the father hasn't the sense of a goat when it comes to his boys. He can't or won't see that there is anger building over their shenanigans.

"Their last go-round crossed the line, George. Those boys should not have driven the sheep onto the rail tracks. 'Tis true, their trick did delay the arrival of the panjandrums from Dublin for the naval review, but the farmers were furious — they lost a day's work driving their flocks back away. A couple of the small holders lost sheep in the trampling, and it took all my diplomacy and some of the McGuinnesses' sheep to calm the situation. The game was not worth the candle.

"And to tell the truth, George, I've not been easy about the reaction from the barracks. The commander had to have been embarrassed, and God knows the English have no sense of humor, so why hasn't there been any repercussion? To myself I'm wondering if they are trying to discover who was responsible before any action is taken.

"All in all, those lads have got to settle down and get on with it."

George glanced away, shifted, re-settled. He looked back at the canon.

"If I can see my way to approach the girl, how do we go about this?"

§§§

George was still standing on the hilltop musing over the night's conversation when he became aware that the sun had separated the sea from the land. The Atlantic was deceptive today, curling and sighing as peaceful as a baby at the breast. To the south across the bay he could see the sinuous height of Ben Bul, and to the northwest the towering ferocity of Slieve League. It was a most beautiful day.

"Well now," he hummed to himself. "The better the day the better the deed. If I'm to accomplish anything, I should be on my way. Whatever the outcome, all the proprieties must be observed."

Calling to Con Dorian as he returned to the yard, he said, "I may be away for a few days. You'll see me when you see me. You know what to do, and keep a careful eye to the house and barn."

Con looked slantwise at George but said nothing. He knew the warning for whatever reason had not been given lightly. There was no need to ask questions. As in any village, any unusual event was made known soon enough.

Con was a dour, reclusive man, and working at George Meehan's place suited him well. It was situated away from the village, so his comings and goings were not subject to the constant watchfulness of the women in the town. No questions were raised about his free time, and Meehan was very fair about the distribution of the work.

Con decided he would have some men up from the village in the evening for cards so as not to be alone.

Meehan stepped quickly to the barn. He began hitching the half-bred horse to the trap. She was a beauty, and he was proud of her. Soothing and talking to her he said, "And wasn't it a wonderful thing that your dam got loose the evening that handsome stallion was visiting the garrison. And didn't he jump the fence like a gentleman the minute he caught the scent of the mare? Ah well, he had English manners. With good timing and luck, maybe we can breed you the next time we have a worthy visitor."

And so with the horse hitched, he started down to the market fair to see what the day would bring. The horse trotted jauntily along, snorting and sniffing the salty tang of the Atlantic. Friends and neighbors waved and hallooed as he passed.

§ § §

Ellen and Catherine had just served the last of the early rush of tea drinkers and were sitting on a small bench behind the counter enjoying their own baking. They could take a short rest for they knew the serious business of trading and bargaining was in full swing and there would be little interest in food until the deals had been struck. As for their handiwork – well, the English would be here at their leisure, and the village women did not buy luxuries.

As they chatted, Catherine said, "Oh, Ellen, I saw the

matchmaker go into the parish house. He was alone. I'm wondering what that is all about."

"Och, Catherine, nothing that concerns either of us. Of that I'm sure. With your fortune and my brothers, we may become the oldest living 'girls' in the parish." They both burst out laughing.

No sooner had they caught their breath than a loud throat-clearing caused them to look up. And there in front of them was the cause of their laughter: The matchmaker – formal, intimidating, and glaring at them. He certainly did not look to be a happy man.

Straightening himself to his full height and screwing his face into the solemn expression he felt to be appropriate, he intoned, "Miss McGuinness, I have been requested by a certain party to approach you with an offer. The circumstances are irregular and the party I represent is of the opinion that a decision must be made immediately. I have been instructed to advise you to use discretion."

The girls sat, mouths agape.

"As you know, it is customary to have prior contact with your guardian, but in this instance Canon Sweeney informs me that he will act in your best interests. If, of course, you are willing to pursue the matter. That is your prerogative. So, what then is your answer?"

This set the girls off in another fit of laughing. "What, what," he sputtered, "Is this respect? Am I to stand here to be laughed at?"

Both girls jumped up and gave quick curtsies. "Oh, sir," said Ellen, "We ask your pardon. It was just..." The sentence trailed off. "Well, sir, I can't give you an answer for I surely don't know who this party is."

"Oh, indeed, indeed. George Meehan of Leiter asks if you are willing to consider a match with him."

The girls stared at each other in silence. They knew him, of course — everyone knew everyone else in the village — but it had been assumed because of his age that George Meehan had no interest in marriage. And what was she, Ellen, to say?

Seeing Ellen's dismay, Catherine quickly said to the matchmaker, "Sir, would you give her a minute. This was not expected. I'll give you a nice cup of tea and bread if you will let us have a minute." Slightly mollified, he accepted the tea and moved away from the girls to give them privacy.

The matchmaker leaned against the booth, nursing his tea and his grievances. This matter was not to his liking. Although the commissions he earned as matchmaker combined with the profits from the small farm he owned enabled him to live with a degree of comfort he would not otherwise enjoy, it was the negotiating and haggling that held his interest and was the center of his life. This business did not call for his skill, nor did it afford him the opportunity to visit back and forth, have a wee drop with the interested parties and strut like a peacock when the match was made to everyone's satisfaction. And God help him if Ellen's father, Peter McGuinness, thought that the offer was initiated by him. The canon had promised, however, that he would be very clear that the match was proposed by himself, when and if it took place. The matchmaker hoped that would be sufficient to appease the McGuinnesses' anger over his role in the affair.

Meanwhile, the two girls huddled together. Catherine, after quick consideration while pressing a hot cup of sweet tea into Ellen's hand, talked quickly and urgently. She knew if the matchmaker stayed at the counter too long, those nosy enough to inquire the reason would draw like bees to honey.

"Ellen, asthore, listen to what I have to say. We both know this is not the match you would dream about, but in all truth it may be the only possible match you can make. If the canon stands behind it, your father will accept it in the end. You know Ellen what your life is like, and it surely won't get better. While it is true we don't know George Meehan well, I've never heard a bad thing about him. He has a good property, and you would have position in the village. Don't say no until you've spoken to the man. I stand your friend at all times, and you know I have only your best interest at heart. Do you now sit a minute and calm yourself while I wait on this woman."

Ellen sat holding the hot cup in two hands that seemed to have become lifeless. She knew the decision had to be made now. Any protracted negotiation would bring the news to her father, and that would mean endless quarreling and bickering between herself, her brothers and him. She knew she would not hold out against them.

The little bit Catherine said had all the truth in it. Since her mother died, Ellen had lain awake many a night trying to see her way out of this trap she was in. She was young and hopeful, but the best future she could see for herself was dogsbody to a new wife and eventually "auntie" to someone else's children. She knew what hell that could be. She'd seen it in other households. Children always knew where the power lay, and doting mothers did not favor a dependent sister-in-law over their own bairns. She would lose the management of the household — no matter that she had improved her father's circumstances by her ability.

She had, it was true, put by a little money from selling her sewing, eggs and some garden produce, but it was not nearly enough to give her independence. In the normal course of events, her father would provide a little dot for her at the time of her marriage, but without her mother to urge him, and obsessed as he was to keep his sons with him, he would never arrange anything. Her choices were few, and she knew that if she were ten years or so older, or George Meehan younger, the proposal would be entirely suitable.

But this was her life, and to what kind of man would she be committing? The canon approved ... Catherine thought she should speak with him ... the matchmaker stared at her.

Muise muise, Mhuire ghrá, what should she do.

As if she had spoken aloud, Catherine said, "Speak to the man — you won't know 'til you speak with him."

The matchmaker had made arrangements, so Ellen was quickly escorted to the snug in the public house. It was early and the business of the fair was in full swing, so the place was empty except for Meehan sitting quietly by himself.

The room was dark with old wood polished by use and redolent with the aromas of tobacco, tea, ale and stronger spirits. Stained glass filtered in beams of red, yellow, blue and green light. Dust motes danced in the beams; for the rest, the room was still with the weight of many years of conversations held in small groups with whispers and warnings and many side glances. It was a place for serious discussion, but not the usual setting for one of this sort. But then, Ellen thought to herself, nothing was usual about this affair. God guide her to a good choice.

As they approached the corner where Meehan was sitting, he rose with a tentative smile as he rested his pipe on the table. The matchmaker made introductions which were unnecessary but formal, as suited the occasion, then turned and left immediately, saying he would be on the other side of the house and that the barkeep would call him when or if he were wanted.

Ellen knew no one would come into the snug at this time, as it was reserved for women with escorts and those wanting a quiet talk — there would be no custom until later.

She sat.

The keep himself came, placed a tea tray on the table, and left. He was a man accustomed to observing everything and saying nothing. His trade depended on his discretion. Also, he knew and liked George Meehan.

"May I call you Ellen?" asked George. With a start, she bobbed her head.

"To begin, I am sorry this must be conducted in such a fashion, but the canon assures me that it would be useless and not in your best interest to approach your father.

"I want you to know, my dear, that if I had not been encouraged to believe that marriage with me would be an improvement over your current expectations, we would not be sitting here. I have seen you and admired you but did not seriously think of making an offer until the canon advised me that he was concerned about your situation.

"I can offer you a good home, and I promise to care for you. But ghissa, my age is written on my face, and you know I cannot offer you youth. And that, of course, is the bargain you would have to live with. I would not keep you from your friends — I know you are young, and you may go about freely. The house and garden would be yours to care for, but I do have a woman now who comes in to help with all that, and she is glad for the money. You have never been in my home, but it is comfortable, at least to a bachelor's eyes. I would have no objection to any reasonable changes you would wish to make. The farm is as profitable as any in the county, mostly from the sheep and the dairy. I would be pleased if you would take over care of the dairy."

At that he stumbled. "Oh aye, that is, if you could see your way to accept my offer. This is entirely your decision, Ellen. I'll drink my tea and let you sit a minute to collect your thoughts. You needn't feel hurried. Your brothers and father are occupied, and no one saw you come in. The matchmaker knows his business. Have your tea, ghissa."

He sat back and offered his cup to be filled. She occupied herself awhile with the tea and then, sipping at her cup, stared blankly at the table.

The sunlight filtering through the window to her right cast a sheen of light on her pale, yellow hair. Her eyes were down, but he knew their color matched the dappled blue of the Atlantic as he had gazed at it this morning. His heart twisted with compassion. It was painful to be young. Thank God the pain of youth was tempered by the hopes born of ignorance, or else where would we all be, he thought. As one grew older, the hope without which man could not live was soon tempered by the pain of experience.

His throat fairly ached with things he would like to say to her. The canon and he had agreed, however, that the offer had to be made as plainly as possible. It was only fair to her and possibly the only way she might accept the offer. She was known to be proud.

The quiet, soft way he had of speaking and the familiar cup of tea had calmed Ellen. The warm sun streaming through the windows called to her mind the last glorious summer before her mother sickened and died.

The farmers that year had gathered and, puffing away at their pipes, predicted dire consequences from the prolonged drought. But the young people were giddy from the hot dry days, the hay ripening in the fields and the air laden with the fragrance of growing things. After the last chore was done each day and they had their tea, they would come by ones and twos to the crossroads. There they would stand, the lads to one side of the road and the girls on the other, giggling and watching each other across the abyss of sexual awakening. Finally one of them would pull a pennywhistle or a mouth harp from a pocket and strike up a tune, and they would form up for one of the intricate, fast reels or sets.

Ellen reveled in the dancing. She was then becoming aware of her beauty and appeal and was sought after by the young men, but she loved none of them and loved them all – sure she was in no hurry to bestow her favors on any one of them. She had years ahead of her. They would dance, taking turns at playing the instruments until even their youthfulness was exhausted by the frenzy of the music. Slowly, one by one they would drift off into the deepening twilight. Reluctant to give even a few hours to the wastefulness of sleep, they would call to each other across the fields until the last echo died away and the land settled for the short summer night.

In the summers that followed she would often stand of an evening by the open half-door and listen to the muffled sound of music and laughter that seemed to rise and hover in the soft twilight. Some of the young people had tried to pull her back into the group following her mother's death, but none of them were mature or independent enough to withstand her father's displeasure when she had friends to the cottage or hurried through the evening chores to join the young people. Eventually she was dropped from the rounds of callers and now, aside from Catherine, she had no friends her own age. Her heart ached for her mother and her youth, and if she wished often for a young husband to come home at night from the fields, it was nobody's business but her own, for she knew it would never be.

She roused herself from her reverie and thought: Any way you look at this, there is really no choice but to take the offer. Her heart had never been given to anyone, and although she had never spoken to George Meehan before, she liked this man. She sensed his compassion and his caring. God knows she had had little enough of that in the last few years. She thought it might work.

Looking up and faintly smiling she said, "Fair enough, I'll take over the dairy."

They sat smiling at each other for a few minutes. Finally, he reached across the table and took her hands in his.

"This has not been the way most matches are made, and you will not have the parties and dances which are usual, but I would like to give you something to try to make up for the loss of the rest. Tell me Ellen: If you were asked, what is the one thing you would have?"

He was curious to know her reply. He did not expect it to be either extravagant or useless. She was, after all, born a child of this harsh region, buffeted by the great storms sweeping in off the Atlantic and ravaged by a thousand and more years of marauders and invaders; prudence was drawn with her mother's milk. Whatever it might be, he did know that he would do anything to please her.

17

She looked at him for awhile and did not pull her hands away. Then, as if she had determined that he was totally sincere, she said, "I want to train for a midwife. Dr. Ward has offered to teach me — I have helped him a few times — but my father always says no. I've been saving my money, and the books and things wouldn't cost you anything." It had all tumbled out in a childlike fashion, but he knew he had won her confidence. He thought it might work.

He opened out the fingers of her right hand, enclosed it in both of his and said, "Done! we have a bargain."

The matchmaker was sent scurrying to see if Catherine could free herself from the booth, and Ellen and George hurried to the parish house where the canon was waiting.

Canon Sweeney was pleased. He knew he had leaned heavily on the need to rid the village of the plague of restless young McGuinness men, but more than that he felt he had united two people who needed each other. This young woman would enlarge Meehan's world in many ways. Increasingly he had become somewhat reclusive, and the canon would welcome George's greater participation in the cares and affairs of the village.

At this time the canon and the doctor solely comprised Killybegs' leadership. They consulted over its myriad different problems without bringing the attention of the English to their machinations, but they could surely use the help and advice of another capable man. The doctor was more than busy since, along with his usual practice, he was often pressed into service when a valuable animal was in need of attention. The canon was on call from early morning until late at night and beyond if someone were dying. Any addition to their self-appointed committee of leadership would be welcome.

As for Ellen, the doctor had often praised her to the canon for her compassion and abilities with women in labor. If she could be properly trained it would ease the doctor's burden and be a blessing to the village's mothers, who were often reluctant to call him when they were in labor.

Along with a tradition of using a midwife to attend a woman in childbirth, there was also the question of cost. Little hard currency was available, so most of the village's business was carried on by barter. Although the doctor never pressed for payment, it was known that he received good payment from the English, and the people were too proud to accept his charity. A trained midwife would be both more acceptable to them and more accustomed to bartering, while the doctor knew he could trust Ellen to call him if a case seemed beyond her skill.

All in all the match would be a benefit to the canon, the doctor and the village. The canon thought the age difference was unfortunate but not all that important. It was a good day's work.

He called his housekeeper to speak with Ellen and see what she might need. She would not be able to return to her father's house — it would not be wise. The housekeeper would buy some few things for her now, and the rest would be bought when possible. Meanwhile, he spoke with Meehan. He told him that he would wring a marriage settlement "out of that auld divil." This was not acceptable to Meehan, who said he was well able to care for a wife.

"It isn't that man, sure I know that," said the canon. "But think what it would mean to the girl to have a few shillings of her own, and you know that her dot is hers by right. Especially after the slavey she has been to those yahoos for these past years."

There was no arguing that point, so George shrugged his shoulders and they reviewed the plans for the wedding. They had agreed the evening before that the ceremony should be performed immediately. The canon had the power to waive the banns, and Ellen and George with a bit of luck would be away and gone before the McGuinnesses found out. The weight of village opinion would be against any objections they might raise, and when they realized that the canon had euchred them, they would have to accept it. They would sulk and the father would surely berate the canon — but that, the canon said firmly, wasn't a thing he was worried about. He was more than a match for the man.

George then said he would take Ellen for some days or a week to Bundoran. It was a resort further down the coast, and there would be inns and shops there. He could not stay away for long but would try to remain until he felt she was comfortable with him. He thought he owed her that.

They turned as Catherine came into the room. She stood and watched for a moment. George went and stood by Ellen protectively as if he expected Catherine to object.

Looking at them, she thought "aren't they a fine pair." She knew Ellen's face and form almost as well as her own; Ellen was tall, slender, fair and handsome. But while Catherine had seen George Meehan many times, she had never looked at him. He exceeded Ellen's height by some six inches. He was broad about the shoulders and had the muscular look of a man who had done hard physical work all his life. He was a fine-looking man, not handsome, with a shock of silvering hair framing a square face with high prominent cheekbones. His eyes were wonderful. They were long and narrow, deep set under black brows and colored the peaty green of the mountain loch. She thought he looked very like the Russians who occasionally took refuge in the harbor when they were driven off course by one of the sudden, violent storms.

When George realized that Catherine was not going to raise any objections, he smiled. His eyes creased with humor and an acknowledgement of the irony of the situation.

Catherine was in fact content. She thought the match would work. She loved Ellen. Catherine alone had been her confidant in Ellen's isolation and despair since her mother's death. Although Ellen's father had tried to break the friendship, even he realized that he would pass the bounds of what the village would accept. Ellen in turn had tried to ease the burden of Catherine's poverty. The love between them was deep, born in sorrow and troubles, and bred by the needs of lonely adolescence.

At that point the doctor entered the study. Canon Sweeney had asked the housekeeper to have him stop in for a word if she saw him. She was not, he told her, to go inquiring. That might stir interest in the activity at the parish house, and this was to be avoided. Quickly the doctor was advised of the situation, and with his face wreathed in a smile he hugged Ellen.

Probably more than any excepting Catherine, the doctor knew what Ellen's life was like. And although, like the canon, he thought the age difference to be unfortunate, he did not think it would ultimately hurt this marriage. The cosseting that George, as an older man, would be prepared to lavish on this lovely girl would go a long way to healing the

21

pain of the years since her mother died. And he knew by the joy in her face as she turned to speak with him that the matter of training had already been settled. For this he thanked God. His practice combined with the midwifery was getting beyond him. He too thought the canon had done a good day's work.

While George and the canon were speaking, the doctor took a few minutes to talk privately with Ellen. He was almost sure this was why the canon had sent for him. Doctor Ward knew that Ellen had been raised on a farm, so his concern was not for her ignorance, but just to have a few words of advice for her and to ask if she had any questions. He thought to himself with a grin, "I'm acting like a mother with her first bairn."

"Well now," the canon announced, "I think we should be getting on with it. Ellen, you'll want someone to be your witness?" While the canon was quite sure her choice would be Catherine, this was said with a question because he wanted the ceremony to be as formal as possible.

Ellen reached for Catherine's hand and said, "Catherine is my choice if she will. There is no one I would rather have."

"George?"

Meehan turned to the doctor and asked if he would be kind enough to stand for him. "With the greatest pleasure, my dear man," was the reply.

The housekeeper came in with a small bundle which she left on the table, nodding to Ellen that she had gotten the items needed.

Ellen had always carried with her the few pounds she had been able to save. Neither her father nor any of her brothers were aware that she had any money set aside. She had always been careful to display a few new ribbons or a cloth for the table, and they assumed that her egg and handiwork money was spent on "foolishness." She was glad she had the money to buy the few things. She did not want to be in debt to anyone, and these items could be thought of as her bridal clothes.

The housekeeper also had two posies tied with ribbons which, by the canon's reaction, had been filched from his prize rose garden. But he smiled resignedly and commented on how lovely they were. She gave one each to the girls and took them away to tidy up.

When they returned the canon herded the group toward the door to the church. It was dark and cool, smelling slightly of incense, smoke, must and beeswax. It was very old. Evidence remained of the fire set in Cromwell's time to destroy the building, but aside from the restored roof and the beautifully carved pews which replaced the original when the churches were allowed to open, it looked much as it had hundreds of years ago. The hewn rock walls were blackened with smoke as if with the despair of many generations. The farthest, darkest corners of the vaulted roof seemed to rustle with the sibilance of ancient, whispered prayers.

Inside the church the canon arranged the bridal pair and their witnesses in front of the altar. The housekeeper and the matchmaker sat in the front pew. The small group shared among them a strong feeling of accomplishment and satisfaction that lent a joyous air to the occasion.

The canon donned his alb and surplice, cleared his throat in the magisterial manner in which he conducted all his services and asked, "May I have the ring please?"

The absolute silence which followed that question left

no doubt in anyone's mind as to the absence of a ring. Excepting the married women's wedding bands, there were few rings in the village. The men couldn't wear them in their work, and there were other needs to spend money on.

George Meehan's face took on the look of a man who has gazed on paradise and been told to come back another day.

The matchmaker rolled his eyes in a spasm of anguish. He knew very well that he would get the rough edge of the canon's tongue for this mistake. But if truth were told, he never really expected this match to take place. It was true the girl was in a difficult situation, but Meehan had none of the palaver or swagger that an older man might use to attract a young woman, nor was it his experience that young women used their brains at all, at all, when it came to picking a husband. It just proved that there was something to be learned every day.

Ellen looked frightened. She knew her time and courage were running out, and she was in a fidget of anxiety. If her brothers came by the booth once and did not see herself or Catherine, they would not be alarmed, but if they came by a second time and the girls were not there, the hunt would be on. If they were to come to the church, she did not think she could resist their demands to return home with them. The habit of obedience was strong, and she intensely disliked the roaring, noisy arguments they enjoyed immensely.

Catherine took her hand and whispered, "Shh, shh, asthore, the canon will fix it. Don't worry."

With a wry look at Catherine, the canon stood, looking like a man who was convinced that nothing would be done properly unless he did it himself. They were all watching him. The pledge with the ring was an essential part of the

24

ceremony, and they wondered what he could contrive.

Suddenly, with alb and surplice swooping behind him, the canon strode to the rear of the church and with a look of smug triumph, pulled the church key from the door. Returning to the altar, he held the old-fashioned key with a ringed top so all could see and said, "This will do the job."

The ceremony proceeded without further hitch. Ellen's responses were given in a faint, relieved voice. She could not believe that the end was almost accomplished. George responded clearly and decisively. Once Ellen was his wife, there would be no more shenanigans from those boyos.

The ancient key presented some awkwardness since the metal loop of it was too large for her finger, but the canon referred to the symbolism of entrance into a new, productive life and advised her to hold tightly to the promise it held.

Shyly, George stooped to kiss Ellen briefly, and the ceremony was concluded.

At a glance from the canon the housekeeper hastened ahead of the wedding party into the house. They followed with the canon. The matchmaker felt in sore need of some stimulant, and Meehan privately felt that a dram wouldn't harm himself either. The canon invited them to share in a glass of his best sherry to celebrate the occasion. Sherry was not the village people's drink of choice, but he deemed it to be the proper beverage for the ladies in the party.

They were a happy little group, but in a little while the canon waggled his eyebrows at Meehan in warning. Both men knew it would be wiser for George and Ellen to be away and gone before the news was out.

George went to Ellen's side and quietly said that he thought it was time to be starting for Bundoran. She turned to him in delighted surprise and asked, "Are we really going down to Bundoran?"

"Aye, indeed," he replied, and was rewarded with a brilliant smile.

Ellen had never been anywhere but the village, so this was a treat beyond her expectations. The awkwardness of departure was overcome by her excitement.

She whispered to Catherine, "I'll remember everything, and I'll bring you back a bride's gift." They hugged and kissed. Ellen thanked the canon, the doctor, the matchmaker and the housekeeper, by which time Meehan was getting the nervous fidgets. He had no fear of her family but did not feel it would be auspicious to begin a marriage following a donnybrook with the bride's brothers.

Finally he was able to guide her to the cart and tuck her few belongings safely away. With much waving and a few tears, they set out on the shore road. The heavy traffic from the fair occupied him for a bit, but at last the little mare saw a way through the confusion and with her ears perked and her head tossing, she picked up her speed and trotted away down the road.

When he was able to take his eyes from the lane, he turned to Ellen and saw her fingers turning and twisting the church key, holding it tightly as if to reassure herself.

"When we get to Bundoran I will buy you a ring to replace the key," George said. And then seeing the consternation on her face, he added, "I know it is your marriage ring and you will want to keep it, but for regular use you will need a band that fits. Don't worry, achree," he said. "You and I will deal very well with each other. I promise you."

He placed his hand over hers to stop their restless movements and asked, "I saw you speaking with the canon. What arrangement did you make to notify your father?"

She looked down for a moment at their twined hands, and then looking at him with pure glee in her eyes she said, "I sent a note home."

A warm breeze blew in from the Atlantic, and the sun warmed their backs. The horse whinnied in joy at the open road. Friends and neighbors waved and hallooed as they passed.

# II

They had been busy in the fields all day. Some threat of rain hovered in the clouds over the Atlantic, so Peter McGuinness drove his sons to finish the harvest. The weather had been fine and dry, but he feared that once the rain started it would continue indefinitely. The hay would not dry, and they would be short of cattle feed in the winter.

With most of the work completed, Peter announced that the rest would hold until tomorrow. As he led the little group toward home, he wished that Ellen was there with her lovely baked scones and hot tea.

He still stung from his recollection of the tongue-lashing he had received from the canon, but in his heart he knew that he had not done right by the girl and belatedly realized that his darling wife would never have permitted Ellen to be treated in such a fashion. Well, peace had been made. The settlement had been agreed, and Ellen seemingly held no grudge. It might not be a love match, he mused, but the girl seemed happy. He was glad of that. It eased his conscience.

When they turned up the lane to the house a wee, barefoot boy came running to Peter and handed him a folded-up note. He started to run away — Peter's humor was known to be erratic — but was grabbed by the neck and commanded to explain his business. "It's from the canon," the little one whispered. "He gave me a sweet and told me you were to have this note right away. Can I go now?"

Peter released his hold and the child jumped like a hare away over the ditch and out of Peter's reach.

As they proceeded to the house, he kept turning the note in his hands. The arrival of a second note in quick succession was a very unusual occurrence. Furthermore, the first note he'd received did not give him any expectation of being pleased with the contents of this one.

Once in and settled by the fire with his first cup of tea in hand, he opened the note but only appeared more puzzled after he read it.

Peter Og, the oldest of his sons, questioned. "Well, what does it say?"

"It only says for me to come to the parish house this evening. The canon wants to speak with me. Now what can the man want? He arranged a wedding for my daughter, told me what her settlement should be and now it seems he has more instructions. I'll not go."

"Suit yourself," said Peter Og. He turned to ask his brothers what plans they had for the evening.

Deprived of his audience, Peter sat fuming. "I suppose if I don't go he'll send someone up here after me." No response. "It could be he needs my advice about something." No response. "It would be rude not to at least stop by. I can always stop into the pub afterward."

"Actually," Peter Og said, "I was thinking of going in myself this evening. Roger Cunningham has a heifer he wants to breed. He was thinking of our bull, and I want to see him about it."

After a short silence his father grudgingly agreed that it would do him no harm to go along.

They walked in amicable silence and parted at the entrance to the public house, where Peter Og had made arrangements to meet Roger. His father went further along and turned into the churchyard. He was met at the door by the canon, who was watching for him. They entered the parlor and Peter was ruffled to see George Meehan sitting by the fire with his pipe and a glass of whiskey.

"Now we shook hands on Ellen's dot and I'm not parting with a penny more."

"Oh sit down Peter," replied George. "I never wanted any of it. Ellen is happy to have a bit of her own and the subject is closed. That's not why we're here." With that he nodded to the canon to speak.

"Peter, I want you to listen to me awhile. Don't interrupt. You know Con Doherty at Meehan's place?"

Peter nodded agreement.

"Well," the canon continued, "It seems he has been friendly for awhile with a trooper from the barracks. The fellow is a Scotsman who took the Queen's shilling as an alternative to the mines. The trooper was at one time a neighbor of Con's sister, who is married and living in Glasgow. This fellow never wanted to be seen here with any local people for fear of any repercussion in the barracks but would go up to see Con when he could. There was always a meal and a dram for him, and he appreciated it since he doesn't get along well with the cockneys who are most of the deployment. He was mustered out yesterday and is on his way to Australia. He made Con promise to say nothing until he had gotten a good bit of road under his feet."

"And what, by all that's holy, does that have to do with me I'd like to know," interrupted Peter.

"Peter, I told you not to interrupt. You'll hear all of it, but you have to let me tell it properly. Well, to continue:

"This fellow, no names mind you, was mucking about in the stables last week when some of the officers were waiting for horses. He thinks they probably saw him but since they never can understand his broad scots, he's of the opinion they think he is not intelligent enough to understand what they say, and he has never discouraged this opinion.

"The gist of it all is the news that the commander is planning a sweep. He's still angry over the episode of the naval review and swears it will never happen again.

"The fleet will be in for the winter shortly, and as soon as they have the ships battened down, the royal marines will be available for shore duty. That will enable Sir Twineham to use his men for the sweep.

"George made the trip to Mountcharles today to advise the lads that this is imminent. They have their plans, as usual, and were grateful for the information."

"And so?" queried Peter.

"Peter, you know the English have never been particular about who they blame in these cases, but they are aware that there is a center of activity in Mountcharles. They've been looking for an excuse to raid. Your two, James and John, have been seen in Mountcharles in the company of men on the list of possible rebels. And, sad to say, it seems that the English have someone who is prepared to swear that he saw them drive the flocks in front of the train carrying all the visitors to the naval review. It's known that Twineham was very angry about that episode and is eager to take some revenge. This is very serious; we must make some plans to ensure that your boys are safely out of this."

While the canon was speaking, Meehan had been sitting sprawled, ankles crossed, puffing his pipe and sipping his drink but watching Peter closely through narrow, alert eyes.

Peter, his fists clenched, was staring at the floor. He looked up with an expression of intense sorrow to say, "Are you telling me that they must go on the run?"

"Peter, Peter, the lads won't hide them in the hills. Not soon anyway," replied the canon.

His face suffused with anger, Peter rose from the chair to shout, "My boys are as good and brave as any Irishman who ever lived. I won't hear another word on the subject." With that he turned to go, brushing away the canon.

"Wait, man, wait. You don't understand."

"What is there to understand? I won't hear my boys reviled."

George rose from where he'd been sitting and said, in a conciliatory fashion, "Ah, sure, listen a minute, Peter. There has been no bad word spoken about your sons' courage. It's not too little they have but too much in the way of daring.

"Tell me, if you heard one of your boys was down with pneumonia in the camps, what would you do? Suppose you heard of a gun battle and knew someone had been shot but not who. What would you do? Suppose there were no word for months and the heart was wrung out of you. What would you do? You know neither you nor your other sons could remain idle, while every move any of you made would be watched closely by the English and whoever in Killybegs wished to curry favor by reporting on you. I know it's difficult to accept, but there are those who have no fondness for you or yours and have no conscience about giving information to the English."

With total misery in his eyes, Peter sat down.

The canon began to speak again.

"You're in a bad spot. These men who are the core of the movement are faceless and nameless. They've given up all hope of normalcy and cut all ties with family and friends. It's the only way to maintain any hope of safety for themselves and anyone who might know them. Even if James and John were capable of being near their home and never seeing it, do you suppose that your other sons would not risk life and limb to contact them? Could you possess your soul in patience if you knew they were near?

"The English count on family bonds in instances like this, and all here know that they have broken some good men in their search for information. If they couldn't track you to your sons, they might pick up one of your younger boys, and even if he held his tongue, he would be destroyed."

In silence the canon and Meehan watched Peter, whose whole body reflected the agony of his heart. There was nothing they could do to ease his pain, and as the canon had many times before, he asked the God he served why so much pain was inflicted on these people and why, dear God, was he so often the bearer of the news.

Finally, Meehan half-reflectively said, "Peter, what does Ireland need? Now don't tell me good brave men and the desire for freedom. I know we don't agree on this matter but there has been enough blood and tears shed in Ireland to make free men of all of us if that were the only need. No, gentlemen, what Ireland needs is what England has in plenty — money. Money to buy influence. Money to buy supplies.

33

Money to buy education. Money to buy food. And last of all money to help those women, poor souls, who have lost their men in the cause and are left destitute with children to raise. And I ask you, Peter, where else but America is money plentiful? And who could charm the money out of your back pocket? No one better than your own, James and John."

"How would they get that kind of money," Peter asked.

"It wouldn't have to be from one person or themselves," George said. "You know there are many in America who are there by necessity. Most of them have managed to get jobs, and a few pennies from each of them over a period of time would add up considerably. Once the trickle was started it would grow. It does need some organizing." He stopped then and started to smoke his pipe again.

With a sigh, Peter looked up and with a glimpse of hope in his eyes asked, "Do you think they could do this thing?"

"None better," the canon replied.

After debating the matter back and forth for some time, Peter seemed resigned to the necessity of emigration for James and John. The canon and Meehan jumped into the arrangements before he could come up with alternate, wishful schemes.

"First thing tomorrow," said George, "I'll send Con down to Sligo to arrange passage for your boys. They won't know him or your sons down there, and that way there'll be no tip-off to the English."

"Hold up a minute," Peter said, "I don't have the ready right now. I was planning to sell some beef when the fleet came in, butt with one thing and another...."

"Don't give it another thought. I know the settlement left you short on cash, as we all are by the nature of things, but I can do this and we can settle when you sell your beef and mutton." And George added, "Don't for the love of God go near the barracks or do any business with the English until your boys are safely away. Your face will betray you even if you say nothing."

"And Peter," warned the canon, "Until the passage is arranged and the date set, perhaps you should keep all of this to yourself. We don't know who is talking to the English, and your lads will never think anyone they know could give information. As far as tonight's meeting, just say I asked you here to form a committee for mending the croppies' cottages. This is true — some of them will be in bad shape this winter without help. And as soon as we settle this matter, we must make plans anyway to help before the winter sets in."

Waving his hand in agreement with the canon, Peter asked, "Tell me, what makes you think there will be time to arrange all this? The commander could pick up my boys at any time if he has a witness. Maybe I should try to hide them somewhere."

"According to what Con tells me, Sir Twineham is on home leave and left orders that the sweep would start when he returns. If everyone acts normally, I shouldn't think anyone would be alarmed enough to contact him for different orders. He's not expected back for a month. Let's try to have the lads on their way in about two weeks. If everyone keeps their head, it will look like as if the boys decided to try their luck in America. Hopefully the English will never realize that we got information about the sweep."

Agreeing that they would not meet again as a group until James and John were safely on their way, they parted with the understanding that Peter would make contact with the canon through George, as it would not be remarked if Peter came by to see Ellen, while visits to the canon by Peter would be considered unusual. He did, it was true, attend church regularly, but to suddenly become a crony of the canon would be remarked upon. If the canon regularly attended the pub, the circumstances would be different.

§§§

The crops were in and the peat was cut for the winter. There was still some warmth from the rising sun, but it disappeared quickly, and the first smell of winter was in the air. This morning the McGuinness brothers were in no hurry to leave the warm kitchen; they sat long after they had finished their breakfast of tea and eggs. They missed Ellen. Although they put a good face on it when asked, there was no doubt that the house and table suffered from her absence. But all in all, they agreed tacitly to each other that she had indeed done the right thing.

Although they knew nothing about the discussion with the canon, the brothers had made some decisions among themselves. They were well aware of their father's reluctance to part with any one of them, but Ellen's marriage caused them to face the reality of their situation. The farm did not function well without a woman to attend to the many details of the house, garden and dairy. They knew that no one would be willing to marry Peter Og if it meant taking on his five brothers as well as the father. And, they agreed, who could blame any lass for feeling that way?

The upshot of their discussions was that John and James, the second and third brothers, were to emigrate to America. If they were able to establish themselves, then there would be further decisions made as to the prospects of the younger three.

When they made this announcement to their father, they were surprised to meet with no resistance. In a manner totally unlike him, Peter merely looked at them sadly and said, "Oh aye, it's for the best."

Since their father had not yet told them of his discussion with the canon, his quick consent was something of a puzzle to the brothers, but it was not in their nature to worry about things that were not immediately obvious, so they soon forgot about Peter's peculiar response.

Though they had made the decision to go, neither John nor James were in any hurry. They were thrilled by their contact with the rebels and were young enough to enjoy the taste of danger without any awareness of possible consequences. And in truth they wanted to linger and romance a bit with the girls about their role as rebels, which to date had merely consisted of relaying a few messages and delivering supplies of food to designated spots.

Peter made short work of this nonsense. To their great surprise, about ten days before their ship was scheduled to sail, they were advised of the date of their departure.

It was in the evening of a soft, dreary day. After their tea Peter stopped his sons from leaving the cottage on whatever excursions they had in mind and gathered them by the fire. With great reluctance he gave them the gist of the meeting with the canon, carefully editing any information that would involve anyone but themselves. He had little confidence in their ability to keep the facts to themselves and therefore only told them what they needed to know — that it was better for them to leave because of a possible sweep in which, so he was told, they would most certainly be caught. They bombarded him with questions, but he would say no more. At last tired of the interrogation, he roared:

"You'll go because I think it's best for you. You'll keep your tongue in your head and your wits about you. There is to be no blathering in the pub. If you're looking to impress the girls, find another way. I'll not have anyone put in danger because of your empty heads."

As an additional safeguard, Peter Og and Thomas were assigned as guardians to ensure that the news of their departure was not public until such time as Peter thought it appropriate. They were also charged with ensuring that James and John did not flaunt their situation as a lure to the lasses. The seriousness of the matter was reinforced by their father's warning that he and their brothers Peter Og, Thomas, Joseph and Michael would be remaining in Ireland and would pay the consequences for any breach of secrecy.

Soon the day of separation was at hand. Although they knew it would come sooner or later, it was still a bitter dose for them to take. John and James would leave tomorrow and there was no expectation that they would ever return home; the journey was too far and too arduous. While the brothers sat with their tea, their father went out, saying there were things to be seen to in the barn. While they knew this was not true, they did not question him. Among themselves they nodded and said, "The da is destroyed with sorrow."

They returned to the matter they had been discussing so intensely, which was the come-all-ye Ellen and George had promised for that night. It was to be a combination American wake for the departing brothers and a celebration of Ellen and George's wedding, belated but long awaited. It promised to be a grand hooley. The brothers wanted their contribution to be exceptional.

They knew that George and their father would have the matter of liquid refreshment well in hand. Good whiskey was not a matter to be taken lightly, and both men were privy to the best available sources of poteen. That left little scope for the brothers' attention.

They sat quietly, deep in thought. Thomas said, "Why don't we get Patsy the lame piper to play. He's the best there is, and it would be a rare treat."

They all looked at him and Peter Og said, "Don't be daft man. You know he never leaves the house anymore, not even to go into the village. Sure his leg is very troublesome, and he can't put any weight at all on it."

"I know that. But listen to what I propose."

So they all huddled to listen to Thomas's plan, and at the end of it agreed it would be worth the try and certainly worth the effort if it succeeded.

Peter Og was delegated to present the scheme to his father while the rest of them worked out further details.

As Peter Og approached the barn, he could see through the half-opened door his father sitting on a bale of hay, leaning against the loose box of the old work horse. This was old Peter's place for thinking, sorting, grieving.

The man had been sitting there for some time. His face was streaked with tears, which he alternately wiped away with the back of his hand or against the muzzle of the old horse who was reaching over the door of the box to nuzzle at his master. Peter would stroke the horse's nose, feed him whisps of straw he was pulling distractedly from the bale, and croon to the horse in a sing-song monotone. The horse was lipping at the straw and trying in a dumb, adoring way to comfort Peter. Although he was conscious of the horse as a warm, sympathetic presence, Peter was reliving the nightmare of his youth, the horror he experienced with his first exposure to emigration.

As a young man during the famine years, Peter had accompanied some friends of his to the south when they had decided to emigrate. Although Donegal had been stricken by the potato famine, several circumstances had prevented the total devastation wrought in the south of Ireland.

His little village had some stability because of the needs of the barracks and the wintering of the British fleet. These circumstances created occasional work for both men and women. There was also fish to be had for those daring enough to take their small boats out to the fishing grounds.

The plentiful trout and salmon in the streams, however, remained forbidden to them because the English claimed sole fishing rights to the Irish streams. To be caught meant deportation to the convict farms in Australia or New Zealand. If the culprit tried to escape he would be shot. Few were willing to try.

Also, in addition to their own efforts they were fortunate to have American Quakers very active in relief efforts in Donegal, distributing food and, in dire necessity, some little bits of cash.

Therefore, nothing young Peter witnessed in the north prepared him for the devastation that was endemic in the towns and villages to the south. The evicted peasants who had been burned out of their small farms for lack of ability to pay taxes or rent were pouring onto the roads trying to reach a city or town where they might find food or shelter.

Many of them died on the road of starvation or disease.

'Til the day he died Peter never erased the memory of the young family they met on the road on their third day out. A young, nursing mother was lying in a ditch with a dead baby in her arms. The young husband, crazed with grief, was trying to pull the woman to her feet. Two small children were clinging to his pant legs, crying for food and their mother. Peter and his friends stopped to see what aid they could give, but it was useless. It was apparent that the mother was past any help. The man said she had been secretly giving what food they had to the children and trying to nurse the baby with only the water she drank as her own nourishment. With tears streaming down his face and cradling his children in his arms, he said he would not leave her but would sit with her until she died, and then only God knew what he would do.

Shaken by the encounter and frustrated by their inability to help, they pooled what remaining money and food they could spare and began handing it to whomever they met on the road. Soon it became obvious that they could not begin to make a dent in the overwhelming need that surrounded them. There were bodies in the ditches, left by relatives too starved and exhausted to bury them. They stopped trying to beat away the crows because the flocks would return as soon as they took a few steps down the road. By then they were cursing with rage and sorrow. The little children caused them the most grief. They could be seen at the sides of the road crouching by the bodies of mothers and fathers, unable to grasp the finality of death.

They met nuns and priests trying to gather orphans from the road. They told Peter and his companions that there was not much food to distribute, but at least they could shelter the little ones they found.

And then they came to the road to Sley Head. There the coffin ships waited for those who had scraped together enough money to emigrate. The long column trudged along the road toward the shore where the ships were lying at anchor. Young girls, eyes red-rimmed with tears and faces white and taut with fear and exhaustion, went side by side with families confused and sickened by the horror around them and the dread of their unknown future. Young men, boys really, tried to hold their heads up and their tears in check. Here and there an elderly person was swept along in the exodus simply because there was nowhere else to go. They were pitiful in their bewilderment. Most of them and many of the little children, already pot-bellied and hollow-eyed from starvation, would not survive the journey. And over all was the terrible silence of despair.

In exchange for the fare they had pinched together, these wretched émigrés would be consigned to the bowels of the ships to share their quarters and miserable rations with rats, bugs and lice. With only buckets for sanitation, they would arrive at their destination dirty, diseased, brutalized and unacceptable. Many more would die in quarantine huts when they finally reached America.

The organs of the press eventually observed that, "In a short time a Catholic Celt will be as rare on the banks of the Shannon as a Red Indian on the shores of Manhattan."

Peter swore that he would never let any of his own emigrate. He also for his entire life cursed the English, who willfully allowed over a million people to starve to death and countless others to die of disease. Although the staple of the peasants was potatoes and the crop had failed, the rich midlands of Ireland had continued to produce more than enough to feed the entire country, but that bounty was shipped fresh to England for the tables of the prosperous. What the landlords lost in rent and taxes they gained many times in profit from the coffin ships in which over two million emigrated. Only God could forgive them, for he never could.

He had never related the story of his journey to anyone but his wife Mary Dugan, God rest her soul. Any attempt to put it into words brought streams of tears to his eyes and no words to his lips.

Despite all his resolve, here he was with two sons about to leave for America. He knew he had purchased a berth for them at a price that assured they would have decent food and access to the decks and fresh air. It wasn't what he wanted for his sons, but there was little he could do about it in this God-forgotten land. If he divided his property, each of them would have nothing or near enough as made no difference. Other than farming there was little opportunity for an Irish peasant in his own land. And as he knew these young bullocks of his to be heedless of any danger, flirting with the girls and acting the rebel, he had little choice but to send them on their way.

They had been given no names to contact. They would be met when their ship arrived in America and instructed as to their role. The canon had lectured them on their responsibilities to Ireland and the hopes that were invested in their ability to do the job required of them. Peter was confident they would do all, and then some, but he wished with all his heart that they could remain in Ireland.

When he saw the condition of his father, Peter Og backed away from the barn door and tactfully began to whistle tunelessly as he re-approached. As he came in, his father became busily occupied with hurling various tools about, shouting that he didn't know why no one but himself could straighten up the barn properly.

Peter Og grinned and agreed that it was a sorry thing to have a houseful of useless sons.

"But listen now to me. We have a proposition to put to you." Saying this, Peter Og then began to lay Thomas's plan before his father.

"Well now," the father said, "It's no secret to me that the lot of you are unbalanced, and now the whole village will know it."

"Och, don't worry about that. Will you agree or not?" asked Peter Og.

"Ah surely, what difference would it make to me. Go ahead with your foolishness, but leave the old fella for me to ride and I'll see you at Ellen's."

Peter returned to the house, advising his brothers that if their father hadn't approved, at least he hadn't objected, which was unusual. They gathered the needed equipment and crowded into the cart for the trip to Patsy McGettigan's.

The day was wearing on as they neared Patsy's, some time having been lost as they stopped to speak to anyone and everyone. All were invited to Ellen and George's home for the festivities, and there was much discussion with respect to the entertainment offered. The brothers would say nothing except to comment that they would see to it.

Patsy's wife saw them coming up the lane and with a great deal of trepidation asked Patsy if he had any notion what the McGuinnesses might want.

"Well, woman, is it likely that I know something you don't know. That would be a miracle," Patsy said.

With that Peter Og knocked at the door and Patsy's wife, endeavoring to smile a welcome, opened the door to the lot of them.

"Come in, come in," she cried. "Will you have a cup of tea? I expect you're on your way to Leiter to help Ellen and George," said with more hope than expectation.

"Well, we'd be glad of the tea," said James. "But we really came to speak to Patsy."

She rolled her eyes to heaven and muttered to herself, "God help us all."

Patsy heard this and from his chair near the hearth, waved his cane in the air and instructed her to get the tea. He further added, "Old woman, will you not be making remarks where none are necessary."

"And haven't I the right to speak in my own house. You be careful, old man, who else would have you," his wife replied. Then, content with the last word, she turned to reach for the kettle.

Waiting until the wife was occupied making tea, the brothers began to tell Patsy how much it would mean to them to have him pipe for them at the come-all-ye that evening. Since they were leaving for America it would be a great compliment to them and an evening to remember.

"Are ye leaving lads? I'm sorry to hear that. I know there are those who say you all are divils out of hell, but sure you're young and have years to settle down."

"Well God knows we will miss all here. But the da says it's time to go, and so we're off. But Patsy, will you come and play for us? There isn't a finer piper in all of Ireland."

Patsy with appropriate modesty disclaimed his virtuosity, thanked them for the compliment and said unequivocally that there wasn't a prayer of his presence at Meehan's that night.

"You know lads how bad my leg is, and even if I could tolerate a ride in the cart, my old woman would throw herself in front of the door. It's hard on herself when I get knocked up with the pain."

"Well now Patsy," they said in a chorus, "We have that problem solved."

'Now now lads. I appreciate your asking me, but I'm old and I know my limits."

"Listen a minute, Patsy, 'til you hear what we have to say," Thomas fairly shouted. With that the plan was outlined in detail to the old man.

His eyes gleaming and his cane pounding the floor, Patsy called, "Sarah, my pipes."

Wringing her hands in her apron, Sarah came rushing to the fire. "Patsy, Patsy don't be crazy on me now. Whatever can you be thinking so. I know you want to be at the doings in Meehan's tonight, but there's no way. I'll stay with you. You won't be alone."

"Listen to me woman. This will probably be a last hurrah for me, and if the lads can make it possible, I'm determined to go. Get me my pipes, they have to be tuned."

Calling on all the saints to preserve them, Sarah went to get the pipes.

When she returned the brothers were busily occupied in the yard, but they paused to listen as Patsy tuned his pipes. While they sat, a crowd of youngsters gathered wanting to know what they were doing.

"Well now," said Peter Og, "That's for me to know and you to find out. Get along home with you now. Your mothers are looking for you."

When the preparations were completed, John and James went into the house and came out with Patsy sitting on their joined arms. The McGuinnesses' barn door, removed from its purpose, lay on the ground piled high with blankets and what pillows the brothers were able to commandeer. They assisted Patsy to his place and then with a heave the brothers lifted the improvised Roman litter to their shoulders.

"There now Patsy, aren't you the Queen of Sheba."

With that they started the parade down the road. Children were flying ahead of them calling to all who could hear to come and see. Patsy had gotten his balance and was warming up to the situation. Braced as he was against the pillows, he blew a mighty blast on the pipes and started up an old tune, a rallying call for the clans.

Wrapping their shawls about them, women came running from their cottages. Men who had finished their chores joined them at the road with shouts of "Up Donegal" and "Good for you, Patsy," accompanied by cheering, applause and laughter from all sides. Patsy, raised high in the air, proceeded through the village, playing the most martial of tunes and attended by children marching ahead, behind and next to the litter. Some of those who were intending to play their instruments at Meehan's that night ran to get them, and soon there were fiddles, flutes, and accordions joined in the parade.

Oh, it was grand.

The women hurried into their kitchens to retrieve the bits of bread, butter and sweets they had prepared to help

Ellen, and soon the village of Killybegs was empty.

Ellen had been busy all day readying the house for her first gathering. Her father with George and Con had helped clean and sweep the yard, and they were now pushing and shoving any movable furniture against the walls to make room for the dancing.

She was standing by the door, admiring her home. Everything that could gleamed with polish or shone with scrubbing. The baking was finished and the kitchen had a lovely smell of fresh bread. The hearth and all the ovens, spits, hooks and kettles had been cleaned, and peat newly laid in the fireplace. It was a big room going the depth and most of the width of the house. Ellen and George spent most of their time there. The small parlor behind the warm hearth wall was supposed to be for company, but few would relinquish for the formality of the parlor the warmth of the fire flickering on the whitewashed walls and the smell of baking and cooking.

Even the canon when he came would not agree to be banished to the parlor but would stride to the hearth bench and raise his cassock in order that his ankles would benefit from the heat. He enjoyed his visits.

Ellen was surprised at how happy she was. She had thought to settle into a marriage totally based on convenience, but they suited each other very well and a day never went by that she didn't thank God for this blessing. She had discovered in the short time they were married that George was a compassionate, caring man. His years of semi-seclusion had made him something of a student of people and their problems. He was often sought for his advice, which he rendered carefully and often accompanied with some monetary assistance. His existence had been somewhat monastic in its simplicity, and every little bit of color or softness which she introduced seemed to delight him out of all proportion. She rather shrewdly guessed that some of his enthusiasm was generated by his recognition of her satisfaction with the marriage. The care and tenderness he lavished on her, meanwhile, was balm to her very soul. The knowledge that she was now mistress of her own home and answerable to no one gave her a sense of security that wrapped her in a warmth of contentment.

While she stood there, half dreaming, she began to hear music. Calling the men to come, she ran from the house to the edge of the yard.

The house had been built on the top of a hill bordering the Atlantic and was nestled against its last rise, facing the east and somewhat protected from the great winds off the ocean. Plain and boxlike with small-paned windows staring enigmatically at the sweep of countryside, the two-storied house had been there for over a hundred years, and the thickness of the walls had withstood the most violent storms. The road from the village zig-zagged up the hill, allowing horses and carts to make the journey. A cleared yard led from the road to the house and barn. The vegetable garden and the flower garden shared the protection of the hill. The view from the top of it was breathtaking. To the west was the great expanse of the Atlantic, capricious and moody. To the north were the steep, barren hills of Donegal, dotted white with sheep. On a clear day the soft rolling hills of Sligo were visible. Late on a fine summer evening, the colors of the setting sun streaked across the sky, reflecting off the Atlantic, creating a profusion of color that dazzled and enchanted. Ellen loved her home place beyond reason.

At first, as she stood there, she could hear only the skirling of the pipes. She called again, "Oh, come, come, it must be Patsy. No one else can play like that. Where is he and how is he walking?"

The men were still in the house, deeply absorbed in a discussion as to the proper arrangement of glasses, mugs and liquid refreshment on the big table that had been pushed into the alcove formed by the hearth and the adjoining wall.

Ellen had supplied a beautifully embroidered tablecloth. George and Peter had assembled a worthy supply of home brew and poteen, and each thought his offerings should have pride of place. After Con had neatly spread the cloth and placed the various bottles, jugs, mugs and glasses on the table, Peter and George rather surreptitiously moved their own contributions to display them more advantageously. This maneuvering in the name of efficiency went on silently for awhile until Con, who was losing patience, fairly shouted, "Give it over now. There's enough for everyone and neither of you has any cause for shame."

With embarrassed grins the two men backed away from the table and turned to follow Ellen into the yard to see what her excitement was all about.

The little parade had turned the last twist in the road and was now visible to the group above. Forgetting her dignity as wife and hostess, Ellen jumped up and down, clapping her hands at the spectacle below her.

George and Peter exchanged smiles that reflected to each other how much they loved her. To himself George thought, "If Ellen is, as Peter says, the image of her mother, I don't wonder the man did not want to part with her. For all that

I've been married only a short while, it would be a sorry day if I were to lose her." She had introduced color where he had not even noticed the lack of it. Her delight in small things was a revelation to him — a lamb chasing its mother, the geese waddling in the yard, the sheen on the coat of the little mare. He had seen these things but saw them now with a different eye.

The rose garden that she had taken over when her mother died could not be transplanted from her father's home, but Ellen had planted as many late-summer flowers as were possible and already had laid the groundwork for what promised to be another impressive array.

The meals he had been used to eating as a necessity were now occasions to be anticipated.

Evenings sitting in front of the fire while they discussed the day's events, with Ellen working at some bit of knitting or embroidery, had become the high point of his day.

And beyond all this, she was so very lovely. He thanked God every day for his good fortune.

Though they were almost winded from the long climb up the hill, the brothers pulled themselves together for a last swaggering effort. Patsy exerted himself for another long blast on the pipes, and the accompanying musicians rallied to the occasion as tunefully as possible. When they reached the crest of the hill, all hurrahed and shouted to Patsy.

"You're a grand man Patsy."

"Sure you could be heard in America."

"Not a better piper in the whole of Ireland."

The accompanying musicians nodded to each other and agreed that indeed the music had been fine. Fond mothers patted the children who had fluted and danced around the improvised litter, then sent them off to play with strong warnings to behave themselves. All in all it was agreed that it was a very successful little parade.

It was a most favorable beginning for a grand party.

The brothers were proud of the sensation they had created. After hugs and kisses from Ellen and a brief "not a bad job, lads" from Peter, they skillfully threaded their way to the corner of the yard, which the young single people had already marked out as their area. With great speed the group broke itself down into its natural components, and having availed themselves of whatever refreshment appealed to them, they all stood waiting, listening to the musicians tune up. This was a very verbal ritual with many interspersions of notes and claims by each talented player in turn that his instrument was the standard-bearer.

"Do ye hear that note now, that's the one. Tune off of that, would ye."

"Go away with you. Don't I know a true note when I hear it. Listen now to this."

The guests accepted these discussions as manifestations of the artistic temperament and waited patiently until they heard the tapping of the fiddler's bow against wood. Having gained the attention of his audience, the fiddler swept his bow across the strings, stamped his foot to the floor and opened the dance with a lively hornpipe.

Patsy was not involved with the little orchestra. It was felt by all that his contribution to the festivities had been brilliant, and he was relieved of further duties until later in the evening. Sarah left him settled in the most comfortable chair in the house with his cronies. As she turned to go, she looked fiercely at him and said, "Mind that you behave.

Tomorrow is another day. Be sure you're able to see it."

"Ah, woman, haven't I lasted this long without taking your advice. See that you enjoy yourself and we'll worry about tomorrow when it comes."

Ellen was at the fire setting one more tea kettle to boil when the doctor approached the musicians for a whispered conference. Having resolved the question of what the most appropriate tune would be, the doctor rejoined the canon and waited until the violinist tapped his bow, announcing "Ellen and George, please." He then turned to his group and waved his bow in three-quarter time. With the last flourish, they began to play, and as the lovely waltz swelled, George came across the room to take Ellen's hand and lead her to the middle of the kitchen. As they whirled and spun in perfect harmony, many of the women stood dabbing their eyes, not neglecting to elbow any of their spouses who were inclined to shout ribald encouragement to George.

Peter stood with tearing eyes. Turning to Sarah at his side he said, "I can't help wishing my Mary were here with me. She worked long hard hours with me and kept the house and bairns as well. God knows why she was taken so soon. Ah my dears, if wishes had wings, I could fly."

Having said that, he put his arm about Sarah and pulled her into the dance. Peter Og took Ellen's friend Catherine by the waist and joined them.

As Peter and Sarah passed Patsy, he pounded his cane shouting, "Behave yourself, woman." Sarah never heard him. Her lovely, soft, wrinkled face was smiling. She had her eyes closed, and for a little while the music and the dance recalled her to her youth and beauty.

The canon and doctor stood unnoticed by the door,

watching the dancers. When the musicians switched to a faster waltz, Sarah, slightly breathless, stopped near George and Ellen to give Peter's hand to his daughter. As George released Ellen, he bent to whisper in her ear. Smiling and blushing, she nodded to him and then turned to dance with her father. When the doctor and the canon saw this, they turned to each other, bowed and shook hands. They were very pleased with the match.

With the formalities over, all the rest who were so inclined felt free to join the dancers. The musicians switched to sets and groups of eight began to form up. The young ones were banished to the yard but did not feel that to be a punishment, as it was away from watchful eyes and allowed a certain license. They could dance very well on the hard-packed ground, and courting couples were at liberty to seek the darkest corners.

With his eyes on the Cunningham girl Tessa, Peter Og had abandoned all pretense of helpfulness and was lavishing his considerable charm her. He had known Tessa since she was a wee baby and he a small boy, but she was her parents' only one, and they kept her very close. In addition to her appeal, it happened that Roger Cunningham's farm marched with the McGuinnesses' land. Not, he told himself, that it mattered. He would take advantage of this event to recall to Tessa's mind the fun they had together as children. With luck, the father wouldn't notice for a little while the attention Peter Og was lavishing on his daughter, and he would make some progress with the girl.

It would have been a revelation to Peter Og to discover how diligently Tessa had worked to catch his attention.

The doctor stood awhile with the canon, tapping his

foot. One of the men came up to speak to the canon, and with that the doctor excused himself to join the dancers.

Catherine was standing nearby. Taking her by the hand, the doctor started to twirl her about the floor. "You know my dear, I was going through the village the other day and I saw you standing, talking with the second Blaine son. How is it that you know him?"

Catherine looked up sharply and said casually, "He brings his mother to me when she has a fitting. Apparently there is to be a big wedding in Dublin, one of her nieces I think, and she has been having a number of things made for the trip. The money is a godsend to me, and I'm hoping she'll bring me more custom."

"I'm glad to hear it's as simple as that. I don't wish to intrude on your life, ghissa, but there is no joy for you in that direction. Listen to an old man and keep a level head on your shoulders."

The music ended and the doctor took Catherine to where a number of the older women were standing dispensing tea.

The old women took it as their prerogative to oversee the refreshments. This allowed them to criticize the offerings, give advice to all the contributors and buttonhole any poor soul who merely wanted a cup of tea and a scone. Their vantage point was exceptional, and they were able to see any small dramas being enacted and watch out the half-door to discover who was courting whom. If one of the women missed something she was updated as quickly as possible by another of the group — it was part of their private code of honor. Occasions such as this would ensure endless cups of tea and interminable discussions during the long, dark winter days as to the meaning of the most innocuous happenings. They were having a marvelous time.

Ellen, mindful of her duties as hostess, tried several times to take over the tea table — with no success. Waving their hands at her they would say, "Go away with you now and have a good time while you can." She finally gave up and did exactly as she was told.

The party was a huge success. No one wanted to be the first to leave. Little ones were trundled to the upstairs bedrooms to join littler ones already lying in tangles like so many puppies on any available bed or rug. Their mothers, avoiding thoughts of the morning chores, children or meals, were caught up in the music, the laughter and the dance.

Late in the evening Ellen, who had been blissfully unaware of her brothers, saw James and John sitting by the fire with Jamesy McGettigan. It seemed harmless enough, and she knew George had promised to keep an eye on them. The brothers had been remarkably well behaved the last week or so, which she attributed to their concern over leaving for America. Neither George nor Peter wanted to distress her with the reasons for the decision to emigrate, so she attributed their determination to Peter's newly apparent interest in acquiring a wife.

As it happened, James and John had exhausted the number of girls who were interested in a kiss and a cuddle in honor of tomorrow's leave-taking. Although there was no question that many were sorry to see them leave, it had also been pointed out to them that kissing and cuddling with a soon-to-be-absent beau was in truth casting bread into the wrong waters.

In search of entertainment, they had come into the

kitchen to find Jamesy staring at the fire with an empty glass in his hand. He seemed in a very thoughtful mood. Their curiosity aroused, they went over to Jamesy with a glass of poteen. He accepted the drink and invited them to sit. Knowing that he would be a worthy conversationalist, they sank to the floor with their back to the fire inquiring,

"And how goes it with you Jamesy."

"Ah lads, I'm a happy man. But I'm trying to resolve something in my own mind."

"Are ye now. And how is it that you've got to make decisions on such a grand evening."

"Well now, it's like this. You know I'm a very old man." To this the brothers agreed very seriously.

"I've lived my three score and ten and fifteen more. This evening I've seen and spoken to everyone I have any regard for. I've drunk the best of poteen. The ladies have brought me cups of tea and the best of the sweets. I've had a dance or two with my old woman and one or two with the lasses. What more could a man want?" The brothers agreed very sagely that there could be no more desirable condition.

"My question now lads, is, "Why would I want to live any longer? If I were to go to my maker tonight, wouldn't I be the lucky one."

Gravely the two inquired as to the effect such a precipitous departure would have on his wife of fifty years.

"I've been giving that some serious thought, and although I know she would miss me, it would be better than getting to be a burden to her. She also has the great grandchildren, and she dotes on them. No, my dears, I think this deserves more consideration."

"We can see your point, Jamesy, but there's no sign of

you dying this evening. Sure you're a healthy auld divil and have years to live."

"Well, my boys, I'm thinking of taking things into my own hands. The point is a man should have control over something in this life."

"Do ye think that? And how would you proceed with the matter?"

"Aye, there's the rub. Now I wouldn't want to be making a big mess. I wouldn't want to have any pain, and it must be quick. Do you think I've covered everything."

"You're a careful man, Jamesy, I think that's the lot of it. Did ye come to any solution?"

"I've been sitting here pondering and I think the only thing to do would be to hang myself. Unfortunately, I haven't a notion how to go about it. The English have the knack of it you know, but of course they've had the practice. I think it's all in the noose."

"The noose you say. And how's that."

"Depending on the knot, things would go quickly or slow. That's what I hear."

"Well, Jamesy, as a matter of science we could go out to the barn and find some rope and practice knots."

"Would ye all do that for me? You're grand fellows. Come along then before Bridie comes looking for me. She keeps closer tabs on me than a cat at a mouse hole."

Sometime after they adjourned to the barn, Bridie concluded her consultation with a young mother who was having "the divil's own time" with a teething baby. Looking about she could not see Jamesy either by the fire or consorting with his cronies. She waited awhile and when he didn't return, she asked if anyone had seen him. One of the women at the tea table said, "Well, Bridie dear, I saw him go out the back awhile ago with James and John. I tried to catch your eye, but you were talking away with young Annie, and knowing what a bad time she's having with the youngest, I didn't want to interrupt."

Immediately, with hands waving in the air, Bridie darted from behind the table and dashed toward the back of the house. Standing in the dark, she paused a minute to see where they might be when she heard voices from the barn. She went quietly to stand by the barn door, unsure as to who was in there.

As she stood she heard the debate as to the efficacy of one knot versus another for purposes of hanging Jamesy.

Wild with rage, she grabbed the old broom from just inside the barn and began flailing at the two brothers, shouting that they were the spawn of the devil and should be ashamed of themselves taking advantage of an old man in his cups. The two brothers, ducking and laughing, ran about the barn. Occasionally they would allow Bridie to catch them with the broom in order to relieve some of her anger, all the while calling to her that they would never let Jamesy hurt himself and it was merely a question of procedure. Finally, tiring of the game, they ran out of the barn.

Dropping the broom, she went to where Jamesy was sitting. Kneeling, she put her arms about him and crooned, "Jamesy, Jamesy, why do you want to leave me."

"Ah, Bridie, achree, sure it's not you I want to leave. But my dear, I'm tired of being an old man."

She looked into his eyes and saw for a moment the young, virile man who had courted and won her. She drew his head to her shoulder and crooned to him, "Ah, Jamesy darlin', and where would I be without you. Haven't we turned the wheel together all these years, and what would each day be without you? Think no more about, my dear, but stay with me as long as we have each other." Taking both his hands in hers, she pulled him to his feet and with one arm around his waist, she led him from the barn.

As they approached the house they saw that the little parade which had marched so blithely up the hill was now reversing its order, and weary mothers and fathers, carrying little ones and urging small boys and girls ahead of them, were winding their way down, grateful for the short respite from the realities of their hard life and mindful of the long day ahead of them.

Several of the young men had rigged a new carrying chair for Patsy and were taking turns bearing him down the hill.

Peter McGuinness stood in the emptiness of the yard. His sons were around him with Ellen and George a slight distance away. With his face gathered into a fearful smile he told them, "Everything will be grand in America. You'll be met at the ship by some of the lads. Everything will be done to get you properly settled. Do as you're told. Ireland needs more than fighting men, and this is your opportunity to help. Use some of the blarney you toss at the girls to accomplish what's needed."

Having said this, he reached out and pulled them to himself. Pressing their faces to his, he kissed each one. They could feel and taste the hot, salty tears which streamed down Peter's face. He reached around them with his arms, and with all the strength of his years of labor he hugged them. When they thought their lungs would finally burst, he flung them from him and strode toward the house, shouting over his shoulder, "Remember your mother and all she taught you. The blessings of God on both of you. Write to me."

The brothers, Ellen and George stood in stunned silence. Although they had witnessed the fury of their father's grief after the death of their mother, Ellen and her brothers had been so paralyzed by their own sorrow that they had almost overlooked the depth of their father's suffering. It had been left to the canon to stand and listen to the shouts and curses Peter had hurled at both God and man. When he had finally exhausted his tears and voice, he never spoke of Mary's passing again, nor did he allow his children to discuss their mother in his presence.

Remembering the nightmare of those days and weeks, Ellen hugged and kissed James and John, promised to write to them as soon as they sent an address, and begged them to use their good sense. She then turned and ran after her father, hoping that some sympathy and comfort would ease his pain.

After Ellen entered the house, Thomas, who had been given the responsibility of seeing his brothers safely to the ship, gave a hitch to his trousers and said, "Right then. Let's be off. We have a long way ahead of us and the da will have my head if I don't see that you are properly cared for."

The brothers shook hands all around and finally Peter Og, unable to control his tears, reached around John and James. Thomas and the younger boys Joseph and Michael completed the little circle, and they stood joined together in sadness as they had been so often joined in mischief. Finally, Peter Og pushed the two travelers toward the road and Thomas, head bowed, followed after them.

When the trio had disappeared around the bend in the

road, George said, "Come. Ellen will have the kettle on, and we'll have a bite of something." Peter Og demurred, citing the chores that needed to be done. But George took him by the arm saying, "What's needed now for you and your father is some hot tea and Ellen's fussing. The chores will be there, and you'll have many long days to sit and think with the winter coming on."

The sun was now well over the eastern mountains and as the men turned toward the house, the bright morning light purpled the western slopes of the mountains, which cast their long shadows toward the sea.

# III

The winter came in raw, cold and stormy. Ellen was expecting her first child, and although she was well, George was reluctant to let her make the steep journey down the slick road into Killybegs unless he was able to accompany her. At the same time, Ellen did not often feel she could ask him to go when there was work to be done on the farm, as she mainly ventured into the village in search of female companionship. And while Con was in the habit of going into the village at least once a week for supplies and a pint, her pregnancy brought on a certain lethargy that prevented her intruding herself on what she felt to be his own time.

She contented herself with their visits to church on Sundays, when she was always sure of an invitation for a cup of tea and a gossip after Mass. George would regale himself with a pint in the public house while he waited for her, and they would return home in the early afternoon darkness, happy to be together. Over their late dinner they exchanged the bits of news they had heard. Once or twice when the Sunday had been bright and clear, her father returned with them after Mass for dinner and would leave after tea.

Peter had letters from America that confirmed James's

and John's safe arrival. They had been advised to travel to a place called Bridgeport, where jobs had been found for them. They had been instructed to settle in, and they would be told what was wanted from them when the time came.

Although Peter still missed them terribly, knowing they were alive and safe reconciled him to their absence. There had been a great deal of military activity shortly after the boys had sailed, and several of the young men in Mountcharles were picked up for questioning. Although they had been released after a few days, it was rumored that two of them were still not recovered from their experience; the English recruits from the stews of London were known for their brutality. Because no one excepting Peter, George and the canon knew the whole story, it was generally accepted in the village that James and John had emigrated because Peter Og wished to set himself up with a wife.

If someone in the village was feeding information to the English, that was the only tale to be told.

One Sunday after church, Ellen was preparing to catch Catherine and ask her back to tea. Ellen had not had a really good natter with her since the wedding – it was almost as if Catherine were avoiding her. But before she could speak with Catherine, her father came to her and said peremptorily, "I'm coming back with you for dinner. Are you ready to go?"

Slightly taken aback, Ellen nodded. She did not think it would be appropriate to invite Catherine when her father so obviously wanted her attention. With some reluctance she walked over to George, who was talking with a number of the men from the village. Catching his attention, she advised him of her father's wish to return with them. With one eyebrow raised, George turned from the group and, taking

Ellen's arm, followed after Peter, who was already marching down the road.

When they were finally settled, drinking tea in front of the fire after a dinner of boxty, a bit of bacon and bread, Ellen asked rather diffidently if there was anything the matter at her father's place.

"Matter, matter? The matter is I've raised a pack of empty-headed spalpeens. They were all behind the door when the brains were parceled out. God knows what I've done to deserve this. Do you know what your brother Peter is about?"

Since Ellen most frequently felt that she would rather not know what her brothers were up to, she sat sipping her tea, knowing she would hear about it either way.

Peter sputtered for awhile, imploring God to witness the fecklessness of his oldest son and beseeching his creator for the patience to bear with such a brainless bairn.

Finally, George, who most often was content to allow Peter to maunder on when he was in a fit of anger, had his curiosity aroused and said, "What exactly has Peter done to upset you?"

"He's daft, that's what. Daft say I, who am his father. Discussing! Discussing! Did you ever hear the likes?"

"Well now, Peter," said George with patience, "If I knew what was being discussed, I might be in a position to say if I had ever heard the likes."

"Oh aye, I suppose you haven't been into the village so you haven't seen the goings-on. You know that Peter is of a mind to marry. Well, it seems that Tessa Cunningham and himself hit it off very well at your hooley. That's all well and good since they're both of a good age to marry.

"But does he come and talk it over with his father like a normal son? Does he think of the proprieties? Does he tell me that we should arrange with the matchmaker to set up a little get-together to discuss the possibilities? No, I say. He does none of these things. Instead, God save us all, he has been discussing the matter with Tessa herself, shameless lass that she is, and they have come to an agreement.

"Now what could I say except that I don't approve the match! Was ever a father so burdened? And will he listen to me? Not a'tall! Oh I tell you she's got him, she's got him. He won't hear of anyone else. What am I to do?"

George was bemused that Peter perceived this series of happenings as an insurmountable problem. He was convinced there was more to it than Peter had revealed, since to George's knowledge it seemed a very desirable match. Looking over at Ellen for enlightenment, he was surprised to see that she was on the verge of laughter but covering her amusement by busily tidying the remains of their meal.

His interest now properly aroused, George proceeded to delve a little deeper.

"So, Peter, why do you think it is not a good match?"

"Oh no man dear, sure I never said that a'tall. It would be a very good match indeed. Tessa's an only one and Roger's lands butt mine all the way to the road. Oh no, it would have been a very good match," Peter said with an anguished look on his face.

Suppressing a sigh, George asked, "Well then, does Roger oppose the match?"

"No sir, he knows as I do that it is a perfect fit. And to give the man his due, he wants the best for his daughter."

Somewhat desperately and with an imploring look at his

wife, who was by this time barely concealing her amusement, George then said, "It's the mother then. She's reluctant to part with the girl."

"Ah sure get away out of there. Why would she object to having her daughter settled next door to herself with the prospect of grandchildren to dote on. No. I say the problem lies with their discussions – ungrateful son to listen to that shameless lass."

"Peter, I swear to you if you don't give me the meat of the matter immediately, I'm going to put on my hat and coat and go down to the public house. Maybe someone there will give me the story."

"Well now isn't it as plain as the nose on your face. The girl refuses to live in the same house as myself. Did you ever hear the like? She's laid down the law to my son and said she must have a wee house of her own. And he, the gormless gossoon, is so besotted he agreed without even a by-your-leave to me, his own father, who raised him and worked to give him one of the best farms in the county. Oh dear, oh dear, sharper than a serpent's tooth, that one.

"To make matters worse, Roger thinks it's very funny, and he's encouraging the girl to stick by her guns. And now everyone in Killybegs is laughing at me. I've tried to get Peter Og interested in the Dolan girl, but if Tessa sees him even speaking to another lass, she immediately rolls her eyes at the lads in the village and Peter goes mad with jealousy.

"Now I ask you: What am I to do?"

Although privately George thought that Peter had brought a lot of this trouble on himself, and even though he personally thought that Tessa showed good judgment in her refusal to live with Peter, it was apparent that the proceedings were at a stand-still and required some intervention. He also felt that it while would be a very brave man indeed who would show any sign of laughter in Peter's presence, the situation was surely providing the whole village with amusing fodder.

Well, this was Ellen's father, and for her sake he'd have to help the auld divil save his pride.

He glanced over at Ellen, but it was plain from the way she refused to look at him and the gleam in her eyes that there would be no help from that direction. Rising from his chair, he went over to the cupboard near the fireplace and took out the last of the poteen. This negotiation, he felt, required the soothing properties of a good whiskey.

Pouring ample glasses for Peter and himself, he sat down again and asked, "And how do the other lads feel about a match between Peter and Tessa?"

"Oh well now, they're all for it. They miss Ellen and would like to have a little order back in the house. I do have one of the women from the village come and do a little cleaning and cooking, but it's not the same, not the same a'tall. Of course it's mostly the two least ones who are so partial to Tessa. She and her mother were very good to Joseph and Michael when my Mary died, and many a day they were there for dinner and tea and coddling.

"Thomas is a different story. He has his own way and is happy with his own company. He'd as soon be reading or working away at his carpentry as eating. And he's shy with the girls, which may be why he's not as pleased as the other two at the thought of a woman in the house — he likes Tessa well enough, but he's content with the way things are."

"Of course," said George, "the house would be a bit

68

crowded with a new bride. I'm sure she and Peter would be looking for a bit of privacy. Were you planning to add on to the house if the match went through?"

"And why would I add on? Didn't Mary and I raise seven children in the house with no problem."

"That's true Peter. But the boys slept in the big loft all together, and Ellen had that little room behind the fireplace. Where do you think Peter and his bride would sleep if, of course, there could ever be an agreement?"

"Of course now, that is a consideration. You're a thinking man, George, and I'm glad to be working this out with you. Truth to tell I never thought that far ahead. I near lost my mind being told so baldly that I was to provide a house for the two 'discussers' — I never looked at the situation."

George sat quietly sipping and smoking for a little while and watched Peter's face as he digested the reality of introducing a young bride into a household of five men. After Peter's expression became more and more comical with each new twist that occurred to him, George finally relented and commented, "Tis a pity in a way that you don't have a small piece of land suitable for a little cottage, but that's the way of it."

"Man dear, that's not the problem. Isn't there a lovely little piece in a corner looking over the main road to town. Mary and I often walked down there on a nice evening to watch the traffic back and forth to the village. I like to go there sometimes even now to smoke my pipe and catch up on the news. Not much goes on that can't be seen from that spot. No, no, the land is not the problem."

"I suppose you and Peter haven't talked the situation

over since you told him you didn't approve the match?"

"And why would I do that? Didn't he make his plans without his father; now he can try to work his way out of this without making a fool of me. And that's the end of it."

"Well, of course it's a big job to put up a cottage and not everyone has the knack of building. I think you're right to be well out of the whole affair."

Peter became very incensed with this remark, saying, "Don't I have one of the best carpenters in the county in my own son, Thomas. Why would you think a little thing like a wee cottage would be any trouble to me or my boys? You're away off the mark, man. And I still have this big gossoon mooning over a hop-o-me-thumb lass who's giving the orders. Now how do I solve that?"

Although George felt that Peter's reaction to his son's intention to wed Tessa left a lot to be desired, he also felt a strong urge to wring the young man's neck. It was obvious that the match itself was not the problem, but rather the high-handed approach taken by the couple. If a formal betrothal had been initiated by the matchmaker with all the attendant meetings and bargaining, Peter would have been in his element and there would have been a favorable outcome.

The two sat for awhile, each lost in his own thought.

Casually then, as if he were off on another subject entirely, George said, "I have heard that Thomas is soliciting a bit of business here and there — carpentry and the like."

"'Tis true, the lad is not anxious to emigrate but knows he must find his own way if he's to stay in Ireland. He's terribly clever with his hands and thinks he might make a go of it if word gets about that he is looking for jobs."

"A little shop with some samples of his carpentry and a

place to do business would be a help to him," said George. "But I'm sure he'll work something out. I suppose being shy he's not a good businessman and difficult to live with?"

"What in the world makes you say a thing like that? Indeed, of all the boys Thomas is easy to be with, and for all his quiet ways no one could put anything past him. He and I deal very well together. I'd like to be more help to him but with all this nonsense right now I can't think straight."

"Well you did say there was a little piece of land on the main road, but if you built a little cottage there just for Thomas that would put Peter's nose out of joint, and of course Thomas would not want to live with a newly married couple."

Peter was very quiet. He began drumming the arm of the chair with his fingers and humming tunelessly under his breath. It soon became obvious that some momentous idea had come to him, and he was struggling to express it properly. Finally, with a sly look, he asked, "Do you really think a little shop would get Thomas started on his own?"

"Oh aye indeed it would. People with a bit of money to spend want to enjoy spending it. They want to sit down and go over ideas and cost. They want to feel that they're getting something extra for their money – a little time and attention. There's no harm in that. It's good business."

"Of course it would be difficult to refuse to build a cottage for Peter and then go and set one up for Thomas," Peter said.

"Oh, that's the truth," replied George.

"Do you know George, I think I see a way out of this."

"Do you now. Well this I have to hear. If you solve this, we can call you Solomon."

"What would you think if I said I would go and live with Thomas in the shop with living quarters in the back and give up the house to Peter and Tessa, if they agree to keep the two young lads with them?"

"Why man dear that's a wonderful idea! But do you think Tessa and Peter would object to having your two lads staying with them?"

"Och, I think not. Peter needs them for the work, and better them than a hired man. And besides: Tessa as I said is very fond of them and they her. She knows also that it won't be forever. As soon as James and John are settled and able, they've promised to send for them. I'm not happy about that but I must say the two in America seem happy enough."

"In that case, Ellen come and hear what your father has devised. I think he's got it. He's as clever as any judge."

Ellen, who of course had been privy to the whole conversation, came and with appropriate exclamations agreed that the notion was indeed inspired, would probably solve the matter to the satisfaction of all, and would certainly help Thomas put his foot in the right direction.

Peter was beaming with pleasure. He said to George, "I've said it before and I'll say it again, you're a wonder for discussion. A wee talk with you, George, and the whole problem falls into place. I must be off now and straighten this matter out."

A look of alarm crossed George's face. Knocking his pipe against the fire tongs, he said, "Do you know Peter, it occurs to me that you as the thinking man in this affair should not bother yourself with details. Why not send for the matchmaker and have him deal directly with Roger? He will attend to all the formalities, and you'll be showing

Killybegs the proper way to do things."

Peter paused with his hand on the latch, turned to the two who were holding their breath with anxiety, pulled himself to his full height and agreed, saying, "You have the right of it. I've been out of my mind with worry, and it's time to get on to other things. Let the matchmaker approach Roger and keep those two moonlings out of it. That's the way. Well I'm off now. Thank you for the tea."

The door closed behind him, Ellen and George stood in silence for awhile. Then quietly she tiptoed to the window and peeking out saw her father stepping quickly down the road. She turned to George saying, "You were brilliant. However did you manage him so well?"

"Whatever are you talking about. You heard your father. He worked it out himself."

"Oh, George, no matter. You were grand."

"Thank you, my dear. But why did you not tell me that this brangle was going on?"

"I didn't know. Oh I knew that Tessa and Peter were courting, but I hadn't heard that they were discussing marriage plans.

"It's never been a secret that Tessa planned to marry Peter. She's said she would since we were children walking to grammar school. Peter was terrible fond of her even then. He was older by some years, but he would never let the other boys tease or chase Tessa. When he left school of course they didn't see much of each other because he was kept busy on the farm and her parents were very strict, but it was always thought that she and Peter would make a match.

"It was only when my father seemed so upset that I realized what the problem was. Tessa is no fool and she'll be good for Peter. They may not have approached it the right way, but I do think they'll be better off without my father living with them."

"Well now," said George, "With any luck it will work out. And I have to say it gives me an unholy pleasure to think of your father perched in front of that little cottage watching everyone go by."

As he said this, he tugged the sash of her apron, letting it fall to the floor. Sitting on the bench by the fire he pulled her onto his knee murmuring, "Tell me again, acushla machree, why you think I'm grand."

§§§

The winter wore on. Peter came and went full of plans for the little shop. Thomas was with him occasionally and whispered aside to Ellen that the da was driving him crazy with ideas — most of them either unnecessary or too grand for the purpose.

Ellen, sympathizing with Thomas while George occupied Peter, asked if they could help in any way.

"Oh no, I manage pretty well if I sit down and go over everything with him. He's easy to talk around, it's just that as fast as I settle one thing, he comes up with another. Soon though the ground will be thawed enough to begin to build. I'll have a lot of help. Peter is mad to marry, and the other two can't wait to get da away and out of the house. Roger promised to bring some men also. I have everyone on notice to send the thatcher to me when he is seen in the area. Once it's started it won't be any time at all in the building.

"I'm grateful to you and George for the push you gave da. I know George won't take credit, but I know the state da was in the day he came to talk it over with you."

"Don't think of it twice, Thomas. You're the one who'll have our father to deal with, and I for one am grateful to you for agreeing to this arrangement.

"But I have a question for you. Have you seen or spoken to Catherine Conwell? I almost feel she has been avoiding me, but I can't for the life of me think why."

Thomas squirmed a bit and, looking uncomfortable, said shortly, "There are some say she has been walking out with the youngest Blaine son."

A look of consternation spread over Ellen's face. "Oh no, she knows better than that."

"Well, I haven't seen them together but there are those who have, and I have no reason to doubt them. Many of them are concerned that she's alone in the world with no one to advise her."

"But where is Canon Sweeney and where is the doctor? They usually keep an eye out for her," asked Ellen with some guilt in her voice. She had been so wrapped up in her own contentment and plans that she had, as she well knew, not made any great effort to see what her friend was up to.

"The canon and the doctor have been worn to the bone with all the problems created by the sweep. They have barely had time to eat and sleep. No one wanted to add another worry to their plate."

"What is this?" asked Ellen. "I knew that some of the young men had been badly beaten, but that was in Mountcharles, and even if the doctor went up to help one day, that was awhile ago."

Thomas rolled his eyes up.

"George will murder me."

75

"Thomas, what are you talking about? Tell me now or I myself will murder you."

"George didn't want you to know any of this for fear it would not go well with you and the baby."

"It's too late now to worry about that. I'm well and healthy and I want to know right now what has been happening that I don't know about."

"It's like this Ellen," Thomas said. "The sweep was planned to catch as many supposed 'rebels' as could be found, including our brothers. James and John were gone by the time the soldiers started their search. Although they would have been taken in, the real target were the lads up in Mountcharles. It was well known that our two left because Peter intended to marry, but there was some suspicion at the garrison that the other lads had been warned.

"They say the commander went mad with frustration. Patrols were sent out regularly to comb the area for any evidence that men were being hidden in any of the little cottages all over the hills. The less they found, the rougher the soldiers got — especially since they were being driven hard by their own sergeant-majors.

"One night they went busting in on a small cottage down by the Glenties where a young fellow and his wife and two bairns were sitting down for their tea. They broke the door and tracked mud and droppings all over the little room. The wife, who was expecting her third, started to cry, and when she was pushed and told to close her mouth the man made a move to protect her. They may have thought he was going to fight, although only God knows how he could have done anything against them. At any rate, one of the soldiers hit him in the head with the butt of his gun. The wife darted in front of her husband, who had fallen, and got the next blow right to her stomach. The soldiers left without getting any help. One of the little fellows ran as best he could in the cold and dark to the nearest neighbor.

"Well Ellen, I don't have to tell you the story from there. The baby was born dead and the poor woman not much better after it was all over. Doctor Ward says the man will recover but his face will never look the same. The two children are staying with their granny until their mam gets better, as we all pray.

"As a result, the men in that area are attacking soldiers who are foolish enough to wander alone, and in retaliation the soldiers are running mad through the cottages. The canon and the doctor are kept busy trying to find shelter for those whose cottages have been destroyed and to help those who are wounded or with pneumonia from exposure."

"Thomas, Thomas, I can't believe no one told me. I could have helped the doctor. I could have taken in some of the families. Why was I not told?"

At this point George realized the turn the conversation had taken and came over. Taking her hand in his, he said, "I think asthore that you have answered your own question. The doctor knew you would want to help, but he also knew he would not be able to hold you to caution. Your father and I have been sending everything that can be spared to help them, and truthfully they would rather go to their own neighbors and relatives, who are more than willing to help if there is sufficient food and clothing."

"But what is to happen now. What about their homes?"

George waved Peter over and said, "Your father will tell you that we have been helping with the rebuilding. Also, the

Reverend Hamilton has been to see the commander and was very adamant in his demand that the raids stop instantly. He knows, as does the commander, that any rebels have long since left the area and it is fruitless to harass the small farmers who are barely able to exist.

"Hamilton is well connected and has approached the Anglican bishop in Dublin to complain about the continued harassment. We're hoping that that will be the end of the raids. If the bishop contacts him, we hope the commander will have the sense to confine the troops to barracks until some of the anger dies down. It's easy to understand that the men in the area want to fight, but they don't have a chance against seasoned troops. It's the women and children who are suffering most. God help this land; the troubles never stop."

"How is it that I never heard any of this at Mass?" Ellen asked.

"You forgot that you did not attend Mass those two weeks you had that terrible cough. The canon asked for donations those weeks, and everyone was very generous with the little they could spare. By the time you were better, canon and the doctor were well organized, and to be truthful I did not want you to be told."

Ellen was very vexed with this comment. "I managed very well by myself for a number of years, and I don't want to be coddled."

"Well, my dear, it is my privilege and duty to coddle you in a case like this. The situation was desperate, and I did not want you in an area where there was the possibility of troops running amok.

"Give it over Ellen. I understand your wish to help, but in this case I did what I thought was right. Your father, the doctor and the canon all agreed that you would never do 'just a little bit' but would be working until you exhausted yourself — and you only recovering from that cough."

At this point Ellen's father entered the conversation saying, "He is right you know. If it weren't that you are in the family way, if it weren't for the cough you had, it may be that we would have told you. As it was, George did what he thought was right and I agreed with him."

Ellen grudgingly agreed that if there were nothing more to be done for the cottagers, she would content herself. She did bring up the subject of Catherine once again, asking her father and husband if they had heard the story Thomas related to her. Both men denied having heard that Catherine was walking with young Blaine, pointing out that it had been a busy time and they had not gone looking for any news from that quarter.

George, as a peace offering, volunteered to take a note to Catherine inviting her to tea after Sunday Mass. "And my dear, if it pleases you, I will arrange to have tea with the canon, if he is willing, in order that you may gossip away the whole afternoon."

Pleased at his offer but still reluctant to concede her point, she said she would think about it.

As it happened, George had occasion to send Con into the village the following day. Before Con left he asked Ellen if she would like to drop a note to Catherine. Grateful for the offer, she ran to scribble a few lines to her friend and carried the note out, apologizing to Con for giving him an additional chore. He waved aside her apologies and gruffly commented that it was time someone took a care for the young lady. This remark filled Ellen with apprehension since she was well aware that Con, for all his reclusive habits, was privy to all the news from the village. There was nothing more to be done, however, until she was able to speak to Catherine herself.

When Con stopped at Catherine's small cottage to deliver the note, the half-door was open and he overheard Catherine calling on God to witness that an artist such as she who could make a donkey look fashionable should not be required to work on material that was meant to cover floors. Con peeked in and saw her wrestling with a huge piece of heavy blue serge.

"Well Catherine, I see you're tailoring a suit. Would it be for young McBrearties' wedding?"

"Aye, and for his funeral also. He would have to wear this suit for the rest of his life and beyond before it will wear out. I appreciate that money must be spent carefully, but sometimes I think if I sew one more serge suit I'll emigrate to Australia. I hear it is warm there."

"Here's a wee note then from Ellen before you emigrate. I have errands to do. I'll be back for an answer if you like."

"No Con, hold a minute. I can probably give you an answer if one is needed." With that she opened the note and as she expected read the invitation to tea on Sunday. "Tell Ellen I'll be glad for tea and thank her. I will see you then on Sunday, God willing."

After Con waved in acknowledgement and turned on his way, Catherine stood staring out the doorway. She knew why the note had been sent. Ellen was right in thinking that Catherine had been avoiding her. It appeared that the reason for Catherine's reserve was now known to Ellen. It wasn't that Catherine wanted to conceal anything from Ellen. But there was no way that Catherine could properly explain to her how she felt, because she herself was having trouble understanding her feelings.

# IV

It all had started innocently enough. One day in the early fall Patrick Blaine had driven his mother to a fitting at Catherine's. He had waited outside with the trap, but because of the size of the cottage and its proximity to the road he was able to hear any conversation within. Charlotte Blaine, a tall fine-boned woman with a long, aristocratic nose, swept into the cottage sniffing as if there were some awful smell to the air. Although the little home was meticulously clean, she looked about as if expecting to locate the source of the imaginary odor. Catherine was accustomed to her snobbery and resigned herself to a difficult hour or so. She needed the business, and she also felt that the way the woman carried her clothes and her sense of style could only help attract more customers.

Mrs. Blaine was in a particularly persnickety mood that day. The gown Catherine had made up for her was almost complete — and, Catherine thought, one of her better creations — but Mrs. Blaine insisted on changing details that had been meticulously worked out in the previous fitting. When Catherine went on her knees to adjust the skirt her customer suddenly turned, knocking Catherine to the floor and sending a box of pins flying all over the room. Instead of an apology, Catherine was berated for her clumsiness and scolded for having misunderstood the requirements, or so Mrs. Blaine said. She also reminded Catherine that the dress was to be ready by the end of the week.

Trying desperately to maintain her composure, Catherine agreed to have all the changes made and the dress ready in two days as requested. Catherine knew this would require working through a good part of the night, since much of the dress had to be ripped out and resewn, but Mrs. Blaine was one of her best customers, and she could not afford to alienate her.

As she swept out the door, Catherine heard her son say to her, "Mother, why were you so hard on the poor girl? I've heard you say that she is a marvelous seamstress."

"Hush, my dear, it won't do to give her a swelled head. One must keep these people in their place."

"Mother dear, I thought they were in their place. This is Ireland, you know."

Quickly out of Catherine's hearing, the conversation continued. Mrs. Blaine turned to her son saying, "Patrick, you know how upset your father is with all of these unacceptable ideas you have brought back from the continent. It was not our intention to have you come back with socialist philosophies. It won't do. Look at your brother, he doesn't think of these things."

With a sardonic grin Patrick said, "No indeed, he doesn't. That's because he is incapable of thinking."

"That's enough, I won't hear another word. You really must control your feelings on the subject. Our friends do not like it. It only encourages these people to think their life is unhappy when we all can see that they are fortunate in their state. Don't I devote many hours to the relief of the poor? Doesn't your father ensure that all our tenants have a decent Christmas? Your brother, of course, will inherit under the entail, and thank God he has not been taken in by your ranting. This nonsense about Home Rule is papist propaganda and you should not have anything to do with such opinions. Be sure you listen to me Patrick. Your father is losing patience."

Patrick did not respond. This was ground that had been covered many times since his return from the grand tour, and there appeared to be no resolution. He had become convinced on his travels that the world was changing. It was no longer valid to him that there existed a ruling class preordained by God to live in luxury and keep the lower class in bondage. He knew how upset and unhappy his parents were with his viewpoint, but he felt morally unable to adapt to what they considered his place to be in the divine scheme of things.

He had approached his cousin Kent, who owned and published the only newspaper in the region, but despite the fact that Captain Kent agreed with Patrick, Kent refused to hire him as a writer unless he agreed to adhere to the paper's policy, which of course catered to the ruling class. Kent's argument was that he had a family to support and was not prepared to espouse the party favoring Home Rule.

Unable to resolve his dilemma and increasingly aware that he was dependent on his parents' generosity, Patrick was baffled and angry. He knew he had to come to some solution. But for now, with his mother's eye on him, he clucked to the horse and flicked on the reins to speed the pace.

The following week Catherine was on her way back

from Ardara. Sometime back, Mrs. Blaine had mentioned her need of a new walking suit and speculated that she would like to have it made up in a lovely Irish tweed. Anxious for the commission, Catherine had gone to Ardara to obtain samples for Mrs. Blaine's approval. The trip to obtain the samples had been fairly simple, since she was fortunate enough to get a ride from a carter going to Ardara and from a farmer on the way home. She had hoped that Mrs. Blaine would offer to have one of her servants buy the selected material when they went into Ardara, but she did not offer, and in order to get the order Catherine knew she would have to go again to the mills herself.

Today she had set out with the doctor, who was making rounds. He took her halfway, and she was soon picked up by another farmer going into Ardara. She purchased the material that Mrs. Blaine had said was acceptable and started home with it, praying that the old besom would not change her mind now that the fabric was cut. Leaving the village, she saw no cart in sight. She kept walking in the hope that she would meet one on her way.

After a few miles the package was getting heavier and heavier, and her temper was getting shorter and shorter. A pox on the old cow, she thought. It would have been nothing for her to send someone for this.

She was beginning to wonder if she would be able to carry the bundle all the way when she heard a horse coming behind her at a good pace. She was at a turn in the road and could not see the horse or driver, but she stood to the side, thankfully placed her burden on the ground and began waving her hand. By the custom of the region, whoever was driving would pick her up.

When the buggy came into sight around the bend, she realized that it was one of the English — and there was no hope in that direction. She turned, picked up the package and, cursing the English and all their airs, began again.

As it happened, the driver of the buggy was none other than Patrick Blaine. He was going at a wild pace in keeping with his black mood and was intrigued to see by the side of the road the little seamstress whom he had privately dubbed the Infanta. Having seen many paintings of royalty in Spain, he had been amazed to find in a little Irish cottage a perfect replica of one of the petite, dark, delicate beauties so highly thought of by the Spanish. He decided to offer her a ride.

When the horse stopped next to her Catherine turned, prepared to be politely impertinent to the man whom she felt sure was going to harass and probably insult her. The young bucks were fond of tormenting young Irish women when the opportunity arose. If necessary she would have to cut across the fields. That would add a little more hell to her trip, but at least he would not be able to abandon the horse and buggy to follow her. To her surprise, it was young Blaine, and he was offering her a ride.

With a speculative look in her eyes, she curtsied and said, "No indeed. If you're thinking of a bit of fun, you're coursing the wrong hare. My feet have served me so far and I trust they'll carry me home."

"Why no, that was not my intention," said Patrick with a faintly embarrassed look. In truth, if it seemed a possibility, he would have been more than happy to engage in "a bit of fun," but he was caught in his own denial and was prepared to act the gentleman. "I merely thought that you'd be glad for a ride considering the size of the parcel you're carrying."

Mention of the package recalled to her mind the miles left before she would reach Killybegs and home. Would it not be reasonable, all things considered, to allow him to transport the material, which Catherine still thought should have been obtained by his mother? Was it not fair to think that this little luxury was due her, considering the many nights' sleep she had lost catering to the old dragon? Wouldn't it be grand to be home with a cup of tea and her feet on the fire fender instead of trudging along like a donkey with a full burden?

Having answered in the affirmative to herself, Catherine looked up at him thoughtfully and said, "Your mother will skin you if she hears that you took me up in your buggy."

"Let me worry about my mother."

Saying this, he reached down for the parcel and placed it on the seat. As she stepped to the buggy, he took her by the hand to help her into the seat.

Both seemed startled by the contact. Catherine had little experience of any male company, and the little she had caused no response in her at all. Patrick conversely had the usual experiences common to his age and class. Nothing prepared him for what seemed to be a shock of some sort. He looked at Catherine to see if she had felt the same thing but she, at a loss for an explanation, was busily arranging her shawl and avoiding any contact — visual or otherwise.

Initially the conversation was desultory, but then Patrick asked why she was so far from home carrying such a large package. Did she not have someone to help with errands?

Lord God, thought Catherine to herself, the man belongs in bedlam. How does he think the likes of myself, scratching out a living from holy terrors such as his mother, could afford to have someone do my errands? She proceeded to enlighten him as to the realities of a spinster seamstress living in a small village in Ireland. Touching lightly on the subject of his mother's fits and starts, she managed a pithy description of the sparseness of her existence.

She intended her comments to be entertaining, but the facts seeped through and although Patrick found himself laughing at descriptions of Catherine trying to fit a suit to a farmer who was tongue-tied at the thought of the young lady on her knees before him measuring the length of his trousers, the rigor of her existence was there to be seen.

When they were approaching the village, she stopped her narrative and asked to be let down from the buggy.

Patrick said, "But I intend to drive you home. It's only another mile."

With an amused smile Catherine replied, "If you drove me to the door of my cottage, within ten minutes I would have all the women of Killybegs lined up and inquiring as to the whys and wherefores of my arrival. And in the evening I would have the canon inquire if I had a right conscience, and the doctor to see if I was in my right mind. Sure you and I are as far apart as chalk and cheese.

"You know yourself how angry your mother would be if she were to find out you took me up in your buggy. It would not be yourself that would suffer. She would take her business from me, and the work I do for her and a few of her friends makes the difference between tea or water to drink. I do almost all the tailoring in the village, but there is not enough of it to support me in style. So then, I thank you for the ride and the company. God's blessing on you for your kindness. And for the love of God, don't tell your mother you were speaking to me."

As she said that she jumped from the buggy, reached up for her package and hurried down the road.

Patrick sat slightly stunned. He knew of course that there was little if any social exchange between the natives and the Anglo-Irish, but it had never concerned him until now. Having become accustomed to a great deal of freedom on the continent, he felt overwhelmed by the realization that not only was this delightful girl socially unacceptable, but that she would probably be ostracized by both factions if he were to attempt see or speak with her.

The black mood that had caused him to take the buggy and race along the roads returned.

For days after that Patrick careened about the countryside. To inquiries about any problem he might have he returned short answers. Finally, after a week or so, his mother told him she wanted to go into the village and, temper or not, he was to drive her.

With a surly reply he agreed to be ready in a half-hour and asked where it was she wanted to go. He was slightly turned away and his mother did not see the pleased expression on his face when she replied that she wanted to see the seamstress about a suit she was planning. He determined that he would find a way to leave a note for Catherine without his mother's knowledge.

Catherine by the nature of her position in life did not have the luxury of indulging in fits of temper. The evening of her expedition to Ardara, however, she did sit a long time by her fire with a cup of tea growing cold in her hands. She could not name what was bothering her but knew that her refreshingly open response to young Blaine was not anything she had ever experienced. The young lads in the village treated her with a polite respect that did not encourage any intimacy. Nor, if truth were told, did she have an interest in any of them. She was accustomed from early childhood to being set slightly apart. This was not because of any property or wealth but from a lingering memory of what her family had once been.

Her Conwells had a recorded history dating from the thirteenth century. For four hundred years and more they had been trustees and administrators of the Catholic church lands in Ulster. The position, barring malfeasance, was hereditary. By all accounts the Conwells' administration had been as fair and honorable as human nature would allow. Within the standards of their time they were sophisticated and cosmopolitan. It was a necessary part of their duties that they trade with people from many countries. In the course of this trade, friendships and alliances were formed. Catherine's very appearance was mute testimony to an international match made generations before.

The young men of the family preparing to take their place as the inheritors of the position were trained in bardic memory. At any time they could be required to recite the holdings and yield of any of the estates in their care. They had to know the families working the land and the count of the animals and cottages. Written records were scarce and not always useful in dealing with farmers and traders, as literacy was confined to the wealthy and the church.

The position passed to the oldest son of each generation, and she was the last direct descendant of the principal line. It was not only the emigration of the sons to friendly lands but the continued oppression of ancient families in Ireland —

who may have served as rallying points for an occupied country – that caused the family to die out.

In 1610 when the English took possession of the church lands in Ulster and distributed them to the Church of Scotland, her family suffered terribly. A family such as Catherine's, with strong ties to the Catholic countries of Spain and France, was not to be allowed to exist. They were left homeless and without any land or trade to support themselves; they were also harried and persecuted constantly by the English. The sons were spirited to abbeys and monasteries in France to be educated as befitted their station, but there was no place in Ireland to which they could return. Those who did were forced to live in the worst conditions possible. The Conwell family wished, however, to keep their presence in Ireland in the hope that one day it would be a free country again. Her father was the last.

Combined with the perception that Catherine was not really one of them, the women of Killybegs also took exception to her appearance. Her slight bones and small stature did not bode well to be the wife of a farmer. She could not deny that she did not have a great deal of physical strength. Of endurance she had plenty, but not the strength to help in the fields, which would be required of the wife of a small farmer. Since she had no parents to provide her with a dowry, all she had in the world was the tiny cottage where her parents had lived and the skills her mother had taught her. This was not sufficient to obtain for her a match with one of the wealthier farmers. With time she had come to accept that she would probably never marry.

Her curious reaction to young Blaine was upsetting to her. She felt that she had come to terms with what her life would be, and she had no wish to deal with the unknown.

Oh well, she thought, there won't be any occasion to see or speak to him again. And thank God for that. She was determined to put the incident out of her mind.

She was therefore annoyed when Patrick accompanied his mother, who was anxious to have the proposed walking suit as soon as possible.

Muttering under her breath with a mouthful of pins, Catherine could only be grateful, for once, that Mrs. Blaine disregarded any remarks that were not in response to a statement or question of her own. The general gist of Catherine's mutterings was a discourse on the thickness of English skulls and their total disregard for the entire human race excepting those born English and wealthy.

Finally, she finished what could be accomplished that day and asked Mrs. Blaine if she could be paid the money she had spent for the fabric. With raised eyebrows and a look of disbelief, the woman replied, "Of course not. Why would I pay you when I am not sure the suit will be to my satisfaction? You may present me with a bill when you have finished, and we will discuss it." She turned and left.

Catherine almost wept with frustration. The purchase had left her with no money, and now she had no hopes of replenishing her cupboard.

Patrick overheard the conversation and was aghast at his mother's indifference to the girl's need. With anger in his voice he asked her why she did not pay the seamstress for the tweed.

His mother turned to him saying, "It is none of your affair, Patrick, but if you must know I do not wish to encourage any pretensions on her part. If she increases her business, I will lose her attention, and it is convenient for me to have such an excellent seamstress available to me whenever I require her services. If I were to advance her money, she would be able to hire someone to help her turn out more work. No, the situation suits me as it is, and believe me she will have the suit finished quickly in order to be paid. The Irish are known to be lazy. One must keep at them."

Patrick was so furious with the patent unfairness of these remarks that he felt he could not leave the note he had prepared. It seemed fatuous and smug in light of Catherine's problems. He would have to think the matter out and devise some other plan.

Try as he would though, over the next days Patrick could not think of any reason to approach Catherine, nor any way to communicate with her. Increasingly he became conscious of the chasm between himself and the girl.

Just as he was reconciled to thinking that the idea of contacting Catherine was impossible, his mother asked him to run an errand.

It was a wild, blowing day. The rain was sweeping in horizontally from the Atlantic and all the creatures in the fields were huddled, heads down with their backs to the wind. When he went into his mother's small sitting room, there was a fire warming the lovely room and his mother was lounging on her chaise. She had not been well for some days, and with concern he asked how she was.

Waving her hand at him she said, "I shall be well enough when this dreadful weather improves. I am bored however, and I want you to go into the village. You know that my suit was to be ready yesterday and I was not well enough to go for the last try-on. Catherine has been very precise in the past and I expect that this suit will fit quite well. Go to her cottage and tell her I'm anxious to have it." She turned back to the book she was reading.

Patrick stood looking at his mother for awhile.

"Do you intend to give me the money for payment?"

"Patrick, please don't be tiresome. I've explained this to you. I will of course pay her, but there is no need to take the money with you. She will give you the suit. What else could she possibly do with it? Certainly no one in the village would purchase it."

"I will not ask for a suit which entailed many hours of work without paying the girl." He turned to leave.

"Oh bother. Take the money. You are behaving dreadfully, Patrick. I'm sure I don't know where all of this is leading, but you had better rethink your attitude."

When he arrived at the cottage he knocked at the door and stood back a distance from the entryway. The half-door opened, and Catherine appeared. He had not seen her in several weeks and was appalled at her appearance. Her lovely, translucent pallor had become sallow, and her face was pinched. It was obvious she had not been eating properly.

Holding the money in his outstretched hand he said, "I've come for the suit."

Catherine looked out at the apparition in her doorway. He had dismounted from his horse, but the oilskins and oversized rainhat in addition to his height combined to make him appear overwhelming. She stepped back and let out a gasp of surprise.

"Oh, forgive me, I did not mean to startle you. It's all right. Mother wanted her suit. She's not well and slightly bored. I have the money."

"Certainly, certainly. It is all finished, but your mother usually requires another try-on." This was said with a question in her voice.

"She said that you have always been precise, and she feels sure it will fit. In any event you can always do an alteration."

"Well then, I will wrap it if you will be so kind as to wait a minute. Would you step inside?"

Patrick, consumed with curiosity, shook himself, causing showers of water to pour from the oilskins, then stepped tentatively inside the cottage. Mindful now of her situation, he was careful to remain by the open half-door.

Glancing quickly about him, he was saddened by the bleakness of her existence. The little room was clean and neat but sparsely furnished, with little regard to comfort. The space was cold and the small fire burning did little to banish the damp. Judging by the pile of peat stacked by the door, it would not be long before her supply was used up.

Catherine was busy with the wrapping trying to ensure that the rain did not penetrate to the suit. Noting this, Patrick said, "Don't be concerned. I have an oilskin to wrap it in. It will be just fine."

She turned and smiled gratefully, handing him the parcel.

"Catherine, Catherine...." He paused, unable to express what he wanted to say. "Catherine, I will be at Fintra Strand each Sunday. If you walk there, we could talk. I know you go to Mass in the morning, but later? I will be there every Sunday until you come. Please Catherine."

Startled, she looked up at him. The face that was so like his mother's looked down at her with a pleading expression. She marveled that the blue-green eyes, so cold and indifferent in the parent, could hold such warmth in the son.

Unable to speak, she looked down and shook her head.

He took the package and said, "Don't say no yet. Think about it, please. I will be there Sundays until you come to me." He turned and left.

After he left, Catherine sat weeping by the fire. Her life was bare and cold, but she had become inured to existing as she did. To be given a glimpse of something she thought was denied her was more than she could bear.

When she had exhausted herself she got up, splashed water on her face and said aloud, "Enough of that, my girl. All the tears in the world won't change the fact that he is not for you." With that she grabbed her shawl from the hook by the door and hurried to the village shop, telling herself that a cup of tea was just the thing she needed. Now that she had been paid, she could buy some food.

It had been a very difficult past few weeks. She was sure that it was only through Patrick that the money came today. Never again would she leave herself in such dire straits. Just this morning she'd determined that she would have to approach the canon for some help. Only her pride had kept her going this long. Because the weather had been so terrible, there had been very little socializing in the village, and she had not been questioned about her peaked appearance. Even after Mass on Sunday people scurried home, glad to be out of the wind and rain and home sitting by the fire.

She had, however, seen the doctor yesterday. Looking sharply at her he asked if she were well. Though she assured him she was, she knew he would soon come to check on her.

Well, thank God she was past the worst. With spring coming there would be small jobs from the villagers — children who were "popping out of their clothes," or some finery for a wedding or two. Hopefully she would be asked to do the bridal clothes for Tessa, when and if they were ever able to come to terms with old Peter.

The following Sunday she attended Mass as usual, but when the last prayer was said she remained in place for awhile. The quiet in the little church was soothing to her overwrought senses. Finally she rose with the intention of latching on to one of her friends in hopes of receiving an invitation to dinner or tea. That would ensure her of an occupation for the long, lonely Sunday.

Outside the church she was surprised to see only the backs of people hurrying down the road, intent on their dinner. Children were running ahead of their parents, anxious to get past the business of eating in order to have more time to play – Sunday was the only day free from school and a heavy load of chores.

She had stayed longer in the church than she realized.

If she turned she could see her little cottage sitting by the side of the road.

As if propelled by a force outside herself, her feet started to walk in the direction of Fintra Strand.

As she walked, she berated herself for her foolishness. Then in the next moment she would tell herself that even she was entitled to a Sunday walk with a gentleman. Then her other voice would remind her that the gentleman was Protestant, wealthy and not interested in a young Irish girl except for his own pleasure. Forlornly then would come the reply: Why can I not be young and pretty and admired for just one day?

And so it went until finally she reached the shore.

As she came out from the overhanging trees, the sunlight

off the water dazzled her eyes, and for a short time she saw only the glare. When her vision cleared, she saw Patrick standing by a pool of water left by the receding tide. He had seen her first, and in his eyes was the light that she thought peculiar only to her mother and father. It had glowed between them all her young life. Although she had been allowed to share in it, she was never able to invoke it, and the light had died in her mother's eyes after her father's death. Tears now came to her own.

Walking toward her, he held out his hands and took hers, cold and calloused, into his. "I wish it were possible to invite you for a meal. It does not seem right to keep you out on this cold day."

"Och, 'tis warmer than my cottage and I'm glad of the company."

"I was so afraid you would never come, and I didn't know what I would do then," said Patrick.

"My good sense said I should stay at home, but my feet brought me here. I'll not meet you again. You know as well as I that there is not a soul in all Ireland who would think it right for us to be walking out."

Since he could not disagree with this, he said nothing but took her arm. They started walking along the strand, happy in each other's company, marveling at the beauty of the day and forgetful of the future.

And so it began.

She swore to herself that she would not return to Fintra even though he had promised to wait each Sunday. She would then miss a Sunday and spend the entire day in misery thinking of Patrick watching for her until the light in his eyes died with the realization that she would not come.

The Sunday after that, out of sight of the village, she would race to the shore telling herself that he would never be there. Breathless and anxious she would burst from the trees and stand frozen as she saw him, waiting for him to turn. It was her special joy to watch his face as he discovered her.

And so it continued.

If Catherine did not appear on a Sunday, Patrick would spend the week wondering if he would see her again, and then he would begin to worry that perhaps she was ill with no one to care for her. Several times he made excuses to ride through the village to ensure that there was no unusual activity about her cottage.

Often he was able to persuade his cook to fix a picnic lunch on the pretext that he would be riding across country with no inn at hand. He would spread the food on a table rock and delight in watching Catherine devour all the delicacies. She blushed when she knew he was watching her, smiling to himself, but the delicious food was such a change from her simple diet that she could not help herself.

The Sundays they were together, he spent his time with her wondering how they could continue to meet and then leave each other again with only the barest of contact. To him it was becoming unbearable, but he knew she would not agree to any relationship.

# V

When Ellen's note came to Catherine, the situation had not changed. She and Patrick could not part, and there seemed little possibility of any solution.

Catherine did as she planned, going to Ellen's on Sunday. She had become very fond of George and was grateful for the happiness she saw in Ellen's eyes. No one knew better than Catherine how little Ellen expected from the marriage — she had accepted the offer as the last hope for a family and life of her own. The happiness Ellen had found was a wonder to her and to Catherine.

Catherine went to Leiter with some reluctance, knowing that Patrick was waiting for her but recognizing that she had to confide in someone, and Ellen was the person she trusted.

Ellen was pleased to see her. Ellen was by nature very private, and Catherine was her only close friend. The two sat cozily by the fire, chatting about events in Killybegs. It was not long before Ellen asked Catherine if it were true that she was seeing Patrick Blaine.

Catherine replied, "Ah now you must know it's true or you wouldn't be asking. Has the village ever failed to report an event?"

"Catherine, Catherine, do you know what you're doing."

"No indeed I don't. Do you not think that I spend the

nights wondering how all this happened? Don't think there's any harm to it. Patrick is a gentleman. But I don't know what to do anymore."

"Catherine, you've got to stop seeing him. You know he would never be allowed to marry you, and there is no hope that it will be anything but heartache for you."

"Well, Ellen, how do you think my heart is faring now? I can't stop seeing him. I know I should, but when a Sunday passes without him I can hardly bear it. I never expected this, Ellen. None of the lads in the village ever caused me to turn a hair, but when I see Patrick I feel I'm a whole other person. What do I do, what do I do?"

"Have you spoken to Canon Sweeney?"

"I'm afraid. Don't I know what he will say — 'Why is a nice Irish Catholic girl like yourself walking with a sassenach?' He'll never understand, never."

"You must speak with him. The whole village knows you are seeing Patrick and it won't be long before it reaches his mother and father. Suppose they ask Reverend Hamilton to speak with canon. At least give the man a chance. Please, Catherine."

"I'll think on it Ellen. Let me wait until I've seen Patrick again. Then I'll go to Canon Sweeney, God help me."

The warmth and coziness of the house at Leiter did little to alleviate Catherine's loneliness. During the week following her visit with Ellen and George, she was almost frantic in her efforts to distract herself. She kept busy during the day with some odds and ends of sewing that came her way, but each night as the village shut down and drew into the cottages all its inhabitants, she felt her isolation more keenly than ever.

§§§

When they met the following Sunday, Patrick looked haggard. Catherine asked him if he were well. Looking at her with some exasperation, he pulled her to him and kissed and hugged her fiercely. At first she tried to pull away, but then she fell against him as if all the strength had left her body.

"Catherine, I can't continue this way. We have to do something. I can't sleep or eat. Meeting you like this and not loving you is more than I can bear."

Catherine pulled away and fiercely whispered, "I will bide with you, I'll bait with you, but I'll not bed you. Fool I may be, but I'll not walk that road. Do you have no concern for my honor or, God help me, my future in the village?"

"Oh no, I swear to you that is not what I had in mind. I intend to speak with my parents and tell them I wish to marry you. What else can I do? They have to listen to me."

"You know as well as I that your parents will never consent. Even if your father could be persuaded, your mother would never allow her son to marry the seamstress."

"But I must try, Catherine. It's no good this way. Something has to happen. I won't give you up. I must have you."

"Fair enough. I will speak to the canon — you will speak to your parents. If we can't resolve it, then we have to part. There is no other solution. Will you agree to that, Patrick?"

Reluctantly he nodded his head, knowing that if his parents refused their consent, he still could not part from this girl, who meant more to him in this short time than all his friends and relations.

As it happened, the canon had by this time heard of the meetings between Catherine and Patrick. Deeply troubled, he sent for her during the week. When she came to the parish house, he asked her in and sent the housekeeper for tea.

"Well, my child, what is this I hear?"

"I don't know what you have heard, Father, but if it's about Patrick and myself, I was coming to speak with you this week."

"Catherine, I know what your life is like...."

"Do you, Father," she interrupted. "Do you know the loneliness and the struggle to keep going when there is no one to care?"

"My dear, that is a condition I live with. But you are young and want more from life. Do you really think you would find it with Patrick, even if something could be arranged that would allow you and he to marry?"

"I truly don't know the answer to that. All I know is that he is the one I want. He intends to speak to his parents, but I doubt they will consent. And if they don't, I've no idea what he can do. God knows he has never earned a farthing, and the little I earn wouldn't keep a pair of cats alive."

"Are you sure you want to pursue this madness? Aside from the fact that he would have to agree to raise the children as Catholics, he would be an outcast from his own people. Would you and he be able to live with this?"

"You know well, Father, that there is no one except yourself, the doctor and Ellen who really care for me. Relations I have none. For me there would be little difference, but you are right about Patrick. He doesn't know what it is to do without. His life has been one of ease and comfort. He has always been surrounded by friends and family. I don't know why he wants to marry me — but he says he does, and that's why I came to see you. I'm not even sure if we can be married."

"Well my child, I could probably arrange for a dispensation, but I would first have to be assured of his good intentions. I imagine he is of an age to consent without his parents' approval, but this will not be an easy process even with his parents' consent. Do you think they will give it?"

"No Father, they will not. His mother will never allow it. I know this, but he thinks otherwise. The only thing I can do now is wait until he has spoken to them. He knows I will not continue to meet him if we cannot work this out. Then I don't know what I will do."

"Catherine, Catherine, give him up. My dear, there is nothing in this for you but a broken heart."

"'Tis no matter, Father. My heart will be broken either way, but I can't give him up. Pray for me. I will be back to see you when I have spoken to Patrick."

After Catherine left, he sat a long time staring blindly at the fire with his hands steepled under his chin. He pitied the girl. Although she said and thought he did not understand, the truth was there were few who understood better than he. In the flush of his young priesthood, surrounded by adoring parents and relatives, he never gave a thought to the future. Now, older, without family, he spent many days and nights bereft of human contact. He knew he was beloved in Killybegs for his stewardship, but with few exceptions he had no affinity with anyone. He thanked God daily for George Meehan and the doctor. They and Ellen and Peter McGuinness were the closest thing he had to family.

The villagers saw that he had a warm house and food served to him, but none of them knew of the long hours when he wished for the softly pitched voice of a woman or the sound of a child's footsteps. Quiet surrounded him. It was not the stillness of peace but the absence of humanity. He did not regret his choice, but it had been a hard one. With his old age upon him, he wondered who would care for him when he could no longer care for himself.

Breaking from his reverie, he shook himself and addressed Catherine's situation. In many respects her situation was bleaker than his. He knew she had little money, and her ability to earn more was totally dependent upon the goodwill of women such as Patrick's mother. He also knew that her freedom was limited by the very fact that she was a young spinster living by herself. She could not of an evening stroll to the public house and find companionship, nor could she with any frequency drop in and visit her friends. Excepting Ellen, the young women she knew were not above viewing these visits as an attempt to interest their husbands. Catherine had been extremely circumspect – until now.

He tried to recall what little he knew of young Patrick. Other than the fact that he had been traveling for a long period of time, Blaine did not seem to be any different than the other young men with whom he was raised. The priest wondered what had drawn him to Catherine.

Well, whatever it was the canon felt bound to do the best he could for the girl. If nothing could be arranged, he knew he would have to insist they stop seeing each other. As difficult as her life was now, it would be unbearable if, God forbid, she had a child out of wedlock. Telling himself that he would try to sound out the Reverend Hamilton as soon as possible, he picked up his bravery and began to whisper the ancient prayers, seeking comfort for his soul.

That same week, Patrick resolved to approach the matter with his parents. He waited until one evening when his parents and brother Thomas were present for dinner. All were seated about the table, which was as usual resplendent with crisp damask, sparkling crystal and beautiful china.

The last course had been served, and Patrick knew his father and Thomas were eager to broach the decanted port sitting on the sideboard. As his mother placed her napkin on the table preparatory to leaving the dining room, he cleared his throat nervously and said rather abruptly, "I've met the girl I want to marry."

The three looked at him in stunned silence. To the best of any of their knowledge he had not expressed interest in any of the young women whom he met at the various teas and hunt balls which were the core of their social life.

His mother recovered first and, prepared to be pleased, asked, "Which of the girls is it? Is it that lovely second daughter of the Nesbitts?"

Gathering courage into his voice, Patrick replied, "No, it is the lovely seamstress, Catherine Conwell."

He had focused his attention on his mother, knowing that in these matters his father would follow her lead. Watching her face, he was appalled to see a look of disgust. Although he had expected opposition, the coldness of his mother's voice as she commanded his brother to leave the room — and under no circumstances repeat the conversation to anyone — gripped his heart with the same fear he had experienced as a child, one who more often than not displeased his mother. He never conformed to the social behavior that his mother deemed desirable and felt less and less inclination to do so as he grew older. Nevertheless, this was his family and he wished very much to have their approval — or if not approval, then understanding.

While his mother sat silently, impelling obedience with her eyes, his brother rose from his chair with an anguished look at Patrick, threw his napkin on the table and left the room.

At first his mother, still wearing an expression of abhorrence, tried to reason with him. "Patrick, this is a passing fancy. You know as well as I that the girl would never fit into our society. She is probably ill-bred and stupid, although not so stupid that she does not recognize what an excellent position she would have if you did marry her. Surely there are other girls you could fancy who would not even dream of marriage, and when you are ready to settle there will be many of our own class who would be pleased to accept an offer from you. Forget her, Patrick. She is a conniving little Irish girl looking for a settlement of some sort, and your father and I will never consent to be bullied."

His father took his cue from his wife and immediately shouted, "It won't do, Patrick, it just won't do. You cannot expect us to support you in this foolishness. A seamstress and Catholic to boot — whatever can you be thinking? How could we hold up our heads if we were to allow you to marry this — this whoever she is, even if indeed she really is after marriage and not a settlement?"

"Father, you know I'm of an age to make these decisions for myself. I love her and want to marry her."

"Tell me this, is she breeding?"

"Father, she's not an animal and no, of course not. I've told you I love her. We started out to be friends and I grew to love her, and I want to marry her."

"Well, young man, tell me how you intend to support her? We would certainly never allow her in our home."

"Why, father? Are you afraid you would discover that the Irish are human and not the animals you prefer to think they are?"

"I'll hear no more of this, Patrick. Apologize to your father and go to your room," his mother said, rising from the table. "I think perhaps you should leave the area and go to Belfast or Dublin for awhile. When you return you will have forgotten all about her and she will have taken up with some farmer."

"Mother, I've told you I am no longer a child to be sent to his room. And I will marry Catherine."

"Then you will do so with no help from us." With that announcement, his father turned and left the room.

"Patrick, I warned you that you would try your father too hard. Get over this nonsense and I'll see if I can patch it up. There are any number of pretty girls who would be acceptable to us, and you must make it your business to find the one you want."

"Mother, don't you see. I want Catherine. I've traveled. I've escorted all the young ladies you selected. I've gone about with my cousin Kent, but this girl is the only one who interests me. Please understand. You can bring father about. I want you to understand and approve."

"Never, Patrick, never! Understand this: If you go ahead with this, neither you nor that trollop will ever enter this house while I am alive."

Patrick turned white with distaste and anger. Flinging his hand out in a gesture of frustration, he overturned a wine glass, and the stain on the damask increased his mother's fury.

"Now see what you've done. Is this what exposure to that ... that person has done? Have you lost your manners, your respect for your parents and your place in society?"

Not bothering to reply, he fled from the room, ran up the stairs, hastily gathered some of his things and stuffed them into his saddlebags. As he passed through the entry hall he saw Thomas, who had remained outside the dining room door and had heard the entire argument — as indeed had the household of servants. His brother reached tentatively for Patrick's arm, but Patrick brushed him away, saying that he would send for the rest of his things as soon as he was settled. He stormed through the door.

His fury carried him as far as the stall of his horse. Standing, looking at the gelding, who was snorting and pawing in surprise at the unexpected visit, he realized that at this hour of the night he was left homeless. He rested his head against the horse's flank and muttered to himself, "Now that was a beau geste — where do I go from here?" After mulling it over for awhile, he realized that his best solution was to bed down in the stable for the night. He had in his travels camped in far less desirable spots. In the morning he would deal better with the situation.

Emotionally and mentally exhausted, he expected to spend the night thrashing about on the straw pallet he had contrived, but instead he fell into a deep sleep and woke to the first sun.

He was grateful that he rose before the stableboys arrived. Though he was well aware the servants knew what had transpired, it did not suit him to have to explain his presence in the stable. He also did not want to encounter any of his family, in particular his mother, although he doubted she would make any effort toward a reconciliation.

Scouring the stable, he found feed for the horse. Tossing

the saddle and bags onto the animal, he mounted and rode out of the stable, urging the horse quickly down the drive.

The morning was lovely. He would ride a bit and think.

Quickly he ran through his list of friends and acquaintances. To his dismay he could identify of no one who would support him or for that matter shelter him against his parents' wishes — excepting his cousin Kent, who was not subject to any social or monetary pressures that they could bring to bear. He felt he needed to present his side of the question.

With this in mind, he resolved to visit the Reverend Hamilton to explain his position and intentions. Since there was nowhere in the area for him to stay, he would ask the Reverend to advise his parents that he would be with Kent. He did not think they would make any effort to contact him, but it was a last courtesy, a need to feel that they did care.

There was also the need to tell Catherine what had happened and where he was going. The distance would not permit frequent visits, but he would write to her. In order to accomplish this he would have to visit Canon Sweeney. To go directly to Catherine's cottage could be misinterpreted by the village gossips, and above all he wished to protect her.

Having a plan for the immediate future improved his spirits, and he began to whistle. His horse felt the change in his master's mood and picked up his gait.

§ § §

Later that morning, Catherine was working by the open half-door and noticed unusual activity in the lane outside her cottage. Several of the women had been up and down, stopping to speak with others they met. Since no one stopped at her door to give her any news, she assumed it was some emergency with one of the children or a "woman's trouble" of which, being unmarried, she was presumed to know nothing. She continued with her work until she noticed that some of the little ones were standing at her door staring at her. When she began to speak with them, their mother came running over smiling, pulling them away and saying, "Don't bother Catherine. Can't you see she is busy."

Since her 'busyness' had never before caused them to prevent interruptions, she began to feel apprehensive. Hearing her name in the sibilance of their whispers, Catherine wondered if she should go out and simply ask what was going on. She was hesitant to do this. She was aware that the entire village knew she was seeing Patrick but was not yet prepared to deal with questions — the logical outcome if she were to inquire about their gossiping.

While she sat debating her choices, the sound of the canon's voice berating some group further up the lane caused many of the women to turn and hasten to their cottages.

"That's right, attend to your home and children. I expect to see all of you at confession this week for gossiping and giving bad example to the innocents." With that last censure, he tapped on the door and entered the cottage.

Mother of God, she thought to herself, I'm for it now. What can have happened?

Fearfully she ventured, "What is it, Father? Is it Patrick? Is it Ellen? Oh please, what is wrong."

"Peace, my child. Everyone is well. We must talk. I suppose the whole village knows what you do not. When the dairyman delivered milk to Blaine's this morning, he spoke to his wife's sister who works there and got all the news."

"And what news is that, Father? Patrick is well you say?"

"He is well, Catherine, but he has had a serious breach with his parents. They refuse to countenance a marriage between you and him. I know this is not a surprise to you, my dear, but he has left his home and gone to his cousin Kent. Both Patrick and Reverend Hamilton have been to see me this morning, and the situation is not to my liking. It's you I'm worried about.

"Hamilton is now on his way to the Blaines to see if he can salvage something from this. He knows as you and I do that while the father may possibly be brought to some agreement, Mrs. Blaine is known for the strength of her opinions, and none of them are favorable in this case. Do you have any notion of what Patrick intends to do?"

"I knew he intended to speak with his parents, but his plan was to be calm and to allow them to accustom themselves to the idea. If they were at all reasonable, he thought he could work out some arrangement and help his father with the ship chandlery and the estate. He knows his father has not been satisfied with his brother's assistance. Something must have gone wrong, but since I haven't seen him, I don't know what to say."

"Beyond telling Reverend Hamilton that he could no longer tolerate living at home and that he was firm in his intention to marry you, Patrick did not say what precipitated his departure. He came to see me to advise me that he intended to marry you as soon as he could arrange something, and he asked me to tell you that he would write to you.

"Catherine, do not pin your hopes on this. If he breaks

with his parents he will give up a life of comfort and elegance. His intentions may be good, but I am wondering if he has any idea what it is like to be poor and outside the pale in Ireland."

"I know he doesn't, Father, and in truth I never expected him to offer marriage. I wanted to be with him and I just accepted that it would end when he realized I had no intention of being more than a friend to him. From what he has told me though, I do not think he has been very happy at home. He and his parents disagree on almost everything. I tried to persuade him to emigrate — that would have solved my problem and his — but he doesn't want to leave Ireland. He has traveled and says his heart is here.

"Don't ask me, Father, I'm sure I have no idea why he would want to give up his family for me. But I will tell you this: If he is determined on marrying, well, marry him I will, and God help the consequences."

Canon Sweeney shook his head and said, "Catherine, you and I know that your family is older and more distinguished than his, but that counts for little in this world. The Reverend Hamilton and I are in agreement that he is being very foolish. This is not any criticism of you my dear, but you must look at this situation. Even if either of you had a copper to call your own it would be difficult, given the question of religion and his mother's opinion of the Irish; but with no means of supporting a family, it is pure madness.

"Think about it, my dear, and God grant you the grace to make the right decision. I'll leave you now. If I have any word from Hamilton, I will send a message. Don't be lured into any gossip about this — I don't have to tell you how any remark would be repeated and distorted. Courage, my child, we will see this through together. If you need to talk, go up to Ellen and George. God bless you."

The Reverend Hamilton in the meantime returned from his visit to Patrick's home. His ears, as he was to tell his wife later, were still ringing from the diatribe he heard from Charlotte Blaine. It was plain that there was very little hope for any reconciliation, never mind approval of Catherine.

Although he felt that Patrick was being foolish, he did think the situation had deteriorated unnecessarily. This type of inter-marriage was unusual, but it was not as if Patrick was the oldest son and inheritor of the family fortune. In other households some provision was made for rebellious, younger sons, either to emigrate or set themselves up in some profession or business.

Perhaps his wife would have some notion of how to mend this rupture. He would write and tell Patrick not to be optimistic. Meanwhile he and his wife would visit the girl and see if she could be brought to her senses.

§§§

The spring passed and it was well into the summer. The long, bright twilights exacerbated Catherine's loneliness. She longed to see Patrick and in the next moment would tell herself not to be foolish. Hadn't she spent years convincing herself that she would not marry? Hadn't she resolved that she could remain independent, not answerable to anyone? But oh, the warmth of the sun, the smell of the ripening hay, and the stream of courting couples passing her cottage in the evenings woke longings in her that she could not name.

Months before she had received visits from the Reverend Hamilton, his wife and also Patrick's cousin. Although she was reluctant to reveal the poverty of her life, she made tea and scones each time and did her best to entertain them and answer the questions she knew were their reason for coming. Patrick wrote to say that Kent was very taken with her and was in agreement with their decision to marry. This would not in any fashion influence his parents' decision, but it was important to Patrick. For years his older cousin had been friend and confidant – the one person who seemed to understand Patrick's disillusionment with the life he led.

Finally, one evening when Catherine had nearly reached the bottom of the well into which she felt herself sinking, Canon Sweeney came. Trembling with anxiety and lack of sleep, she asked him to be seated while she made a pot of tea. Noting her condition, he came to her and took her hands in his saying, "Oh my dear, you have had a bad time, but the matter has been resolved. Not as well as I would wish for you, but I know you are not thinking of the future."

"Tell me please Father, anything is better than waiting."

"The wedding can take place."

That statement drained the color from Catherine's face. Grasping her by the elbow, Canon Sweeney eased her into a chair. Pulling another up beside her, he patted her hand and began to relate the history of the negotiations.

"After the reverend and his wife visited you, they spoke with Mr. and Mrs. Blaine. Hamilton felt and conveyed to them that they were being unduly harsh in this matter. He explained to them that you were a descendant of a fine old family, and that although you had no property, you work very hard to maintain yourself with no family to assist you. He tried to convince them that the marriage proposal was Patrick's wish and you had not persuaded him into it. He told them that your manners left nothing to be desired and if you did not have the education of a young lady of Patrick's class, it was his opinion that your manifest intelligence would soon compensate for any lack in that area.

"He said many more things of this nature, but sadly enough nothing seemed to pierce their resolve to disown Patrick. When he realized that persuasion would avail nothing, Hamilton began to correspond with Kent. The captain had already expressed to his aunt and uncle that he could see no reason why they would forbid the match, but he met with the same hostility.

"At this point it was all anyone could do to restrain Patrick from coming to carry you off with no plan for the future. Fortunately, before he could act rashly, Kent and the reverend combined to pressure the Blaines into a settlement by pointing out to them that their friends and neighbors would be appalled to know that they had cast out their son with no means of support. For even if most of them would agree that the marriage was not desirable, there still is the question of family.

"The settlement they have agreed to is small. Less by far than it would have been his by inheritance, but sufficient for you to live, although not nearly in the comfort to which Patrick is accustomed.

"You are to have a small plantation as soon as the crops are in and the present tenant farmer is relocated. This will be deeded to Patrick along with a small sum of money and all his personal belongings.

"It is less than I had hoped for — not for you my dear, because it is by far more than you presently have — but for Patrick's sake. This is not a life to which he was born,

Catherine, and it will be very difficult for him. I pray you don't end with a broken heart. I am sorry that you were left in ignorance of the proceedings, but many times it seemed as if the only conclusion would be for you and Patrick to give up this plan and go your separate ways. There is only starvation in Ireland for those who have no place."

"I am content father. For me it is more than enough. 'Tis true what you say about Patrick. I know he has no notion of what it is to work hard just to exist. But you know I'm convinced he is prepared to do something wild if we do not marry. He has been restless and unhappy for a long time now. If he didn't choose to marry me, I think he would take another road — perhaps easier but not as worthy of himself. Somehow, some way we will make it work. He is a good man, father."

"I know that Catherine. It will be difficult, but let's leave it now in God's hands. Patrick will soon complete the settlement with his parents. Hamilton will have them meet at the manse. I think it better if you are not there, but Ellen will have Patrick stay with them for a few days, and you can make plans for the wedding. I've told Ellen that she must see you are chaperoned. I will not have anything contrary said about you or him. You will be receiving a letter from him.

"Goodbye for now. Be assured you are in my prayers."

The days passed quickly for Catherine after the canon's visit. She used what little money she had to make some bridal clothes and linens for her future home. She knew now where it was to be. She also knew that it was not a prosperous holding, but it was agreed that the cottage would be repaired, fitted out and stocked with animals. The property of Drumbarity adjoined Leiter, and they would be neighbors of Ellen and George. She was very grateful for this, knowing that Patrick would need all the help he could get, and George would be most generous.

The day of the wedding arrived. It was a quiet ceremony in the parish house since Patrick was not Catholic. Ellen's father gave Catherine away, and Ellen and Captain Kent were witnesses. They all returned to Ellen's, where her brothers and Tessa had been charged with the responsibility of caring for Ellen and George's baby son and doing final preparations of the meal Ellen had prepared. When the little wedding party arrived at the house, they were greeted by Ellen's brothers, who were rather sheepishly smoking by the barn. Ellen looked questioningly at them but hurried into the house when she heard the baby cry.

To her surprise she was greeted by a bedraggled Tessa, who surrendered the baby to her with relief. It seemed that the little one had wakened to be fed much sooner than anticipated, and although initially he was content to be rocked or walked, he became more and more frantic with the realization that Tessa was not the source of food for which he was searching. Since he was very determined, Tessa had suffered some deterioration of her Sunday best and, as she put it, "Those cowardly men had up and left her to deal alone with the situation." There was no question that Peter Og would pay for his desertion.

Ellen took the baby into the little room behind the hearth to satisfy his hunger. George followed to see if there was anything needed and stood smiling at them for awhile. Then mindful of his duties as host, he returned to the party.

There was some stiffness as the group entered the big kitchen, but there was also the smell of good things to eat, and Kent produced from his saddlebags several bottles of claret. This was a rare treat, and the women were pleased. Canon Sweeney examined the bottles and sighed in anticipation of a fine wine.

The glasses were filled for a toast. The baby and Ellen joined them. Any differences were forgotten, and the party warmed up. Peter told some of the more hair-raising stories about his sons, and George contributed stories he had heard about Peter. Con had some sly comments about George's little mare, and Canon Sweeney recited poetry with appropriate gestures and much applause. Tessa and Ellen sang for them, and to everyone's surprise Patrick and his cousin had a repertoire of all the newest songs from America. Finally, when Ellen rose to start another round of tea and food, Patrick nodded to Catherine, and they prepared to go, leaving the party to continue without them.

George accompanied them to the gate, making sure that Patrick had the wherewithal to light the ritual hearth fire. He said that Con had been down to the cottage that morning to ensure that all was well. He wished them health and happiness and turned back to the house.

With their arms about each other Catherine and Patrick walked the short distance to their cottage. It was set on a rise above a well traveled road but was approached from a side road, affording them maximum privacy with easy access to the village. Catherine was glad of this because she wanted to continue to earn what she could from her sewing.

Dusk was gathering as they reached the cottage, and Patrick left the half-door open as he knelt to light the fire. Catherine stood by it, listening to the last song of the birds as they settled. Faint stars began to appear as she saw the first flickers of firelight on the walls of the cottage.

Closing the door, she turned to Patrick as he reached out for her. She walked into his embrace, and they stood rocking in each other's arms for warmth and comfort until she lifted her face to him and he bent his mouth to hers. The peat caught and tongues of light entered the dark corners of the room. The pungent, sweet smell of the fire filled the place.

# VI

Many years later, Catherine stood by the same door anxiously looking out for Patrick. A billowing, blowing wall of white obscured everything and gave noisy life to the small sheds and farm implements in the yard. As she stood she heard the hollow clip-clopping of a horse carefully picking its way through the thick, drenching fog. A moment later she saw the halo of light from a lantern held high. She knew it was George driving Ellen to a young woman who was due to deliver her first child.

Many and many a night she had heard the two of them, roused from their warm bed, intent on reaching the cottage where some expectant mother waited for Ellen. Her skill was widely known, and women who had had trouble with previous births often asked her to come long distances to assist them. If it were at all possible, she tried to help them. If it was, as on this night, a journey to a poor cottage, they would arrive with a cartload of needful items.

Catherine knew Ellen was worried about this birth. She expected it to be a long, difficult delivery, and she was not sure if the poor, undernourished girl had the strength to live through it. Dear God, thought Catherine, I must remember the poor child and her baby in my prayers tonight.

She continued to stand, with the light from the fire

behind her, and as she stood staring at the milky fog, she recalled that first year of her marriage. In the delight of their love for each other, they passed the first winter learning to know each other. Their days were spent absorbing what knowledge they could from George and Con of farm life and the care of animals. Patrick had to be shown how to do each chore. It did not come easily to him who had never worked as a laborer in his life. He was good humored, however, and George and Con had the patience of saints.

She treasured the memory of those nights when the work was finished and Patrick would come in to whatever supper she had contrived. After their meal he would pick up the book he was reading and recite aloud to her while she tidied. When he tired of that they would sit, wrapped in each other's arms, and stare dreamily at the fire. Patrick would recall snippets of poetry and recite those to her. As it grew late and all danger of casual callers passed, they would go to their bed, and those were the best memories of all. No matter what the years brought, that time bonded them as one, and she could never forget the wonder of it.

That first winter passed all too quickly though, and the realities of plowing and working the fields began. Patrick would stumble home at night so weary and sore she had to coax him to eat. Then, as he sat drooping over the remains of his supper, she would rouse him to go to his bed. Sometimes he would rest his head on her breast and weep for his ignorance and ineptness.

What could be done in an hour took him two and three times as long. Many nights his beautiful, graceful hands were cut and bleeding. Her heart broke for him, but there was little she could do beyond rubbing his sore body and telling him she loved him.

It was his opinion that his parents were convinced he would give up and return home. If he did this, of course, they would expect him to return without Catherine. She was aware of this and at times would implore him not to leave her. He swore to Catherine time and again that he never would. The pain to his body was less, he said, than the bleakness and despair he suffered before he met her.

They survived that first brutal year and Patrick became more adept as time passed, but he never acquired the easy rhythm of those born to manual labor. Catherine worked whenever she could, sewing and mending for those who came to her. They did not have any luxuries, but Patrick seemed content with their lot. And while she had Patrick, Catherine asked for nothing else.

Their first child was born the year after their wedding. On a beautiful late spring morning with a bright sun and warm breezes, with the young lambs skipping on the hills and the little children intoxicated by the freedom from their cast-off winter clothes, Catherine went into labor.

She waited as long as she could, but finally the pains became too severe to hide. Patrick looked astonished that she could be in such distress. Despite her protests, he went running for the doctor. After questioning Patrick as to the progress of Catherine's labor, the doctor gave him a wry look but accompanied him back to the cottage.

The doctor spoke with Catherine and assured her that he did not mind having been called before it was necessary. He then took Patrick aside and said that it promised to be a long labor. He did not foresee any real problem, but she was small-boned and he could do nothing except let nature take its course. The doctor said he would stop by Ellen's and arrange for her to come and stay with Catherine.

"She has a natural talent for midwifery and has learned just about everything I can teach her. The women are calling on her more frequently than they send for me. I'm glad of this, for it gives me more time for those who are seriously ill, but also because I know how eager Ellen was to pursue the art of midwifery. And having the confidence of the women means a great deal to her. She will know if there is any need to send for me and will take very good care of Catherine."

Ellen came as soon as she was able to leave her youngest son with Tessa. They got along famously, and Ellen knew she would not be anxious about him. When she arrived at the cottage her first concern was to banish Patrick – his nervous pacing and constant inquiries as to how his wife was feeling were obviously doing Catherine no good at all. Chasing him out, she said, "Go on about your chores. When you've finished, go up and see George and Con. Don't come back until I send for you. There is nothing you can do here."

When he tried to take exception to her orders, she picked up his coat and handed it to him. At that point Catherine let a low moan escape. With a terrified look on his face, Patrick departed.

Ellen went to Catherine and, holding her firmly about her waist, began to walk up and down the room. When it seemed Catherine was too tired to continue, she allowed her to rest for awhile. When Catherine caught her breath, she began to apologize to Ellen for being such a trouble.

"Whisht, asthore, and who would stay with you this long day if not myself," said Ellen.

"Well you know Ellen, Patrick had no idea what to do,"

Catherine confided. "And sure no man has any notion of what it is to birth a child."

"And this is even more true of himself," Ellen replied, "who was raised in a house where everyone lived behind their own closed door. Think no more about it but concentrate on your baby. You have a hard day's work ahead of you, but you will be fine." With that remark she pulled Catherine to her feet and again started the endless pacing.

It was a long day. The doctor looked in several times to confirm what he had thought – it would be a slow labor but there did not seem to be any problems.

At last, when the sun was sinking into the sea and Catherine's strength seemed almost exhausted, the baby was born. After taking care of the newborn and making Catherine comfortable, Ellen went out to the yard where Con had made himself a nest in some straw and told him to send Patrick down. Con stretched himself and started on his way, commenting, "I've never seen anyone in such a stew as himself. Has the man never heard anything about birthing?"

"Ah well, Con, he's led a different life. It's not his fault if everything was covered up and hidden. It's the way these things are done if the money is available. Go on with you now, Catherine won't sleep until she has seen him."

Shortly thereafter Patrick came pell mell down the hill and rushed breathless into the room, calling his wife's name.

She smiled at him. "We have a healthy son, thank God."

Patrick was beside himself with joy. He was so relieved that both Catherine and the baby were well that Ellen thought he would never let her home to get some rest. Finally, after leaving instructions for the night and promising to return in the morning, she managed to escape.

Sitting by the side of the bed, he held the baby tentatively in his arms and told Catherine how pleased he thought his parents would be to hear about a grandson. Although Catherine had reservations, she said nothing, hoping that he was right.

Patrick sent a note to his parents the next day. The note was full of the pride and joy he felt for his baby son and the love he had for his wife.

There was no reply to his message.

Shortly after the birth Patrick heard that his brother Thomas was to be married. He was surprised, not only because Thomas had never expressed interest in any of the young women who had tried to attract his attention, but also because the bride-to-be was the same quiet young girl who had frequently been suggested as an appropriate match for himself. Patrick knew her to be a pleasant, well-brought-up young lady but somewhat on the dull side and rather young for Thomas, who was older than Patrick by some ten years. He surmised that his parents insisted Thomas marry in order that there be an heir to their properties.

§§§

As Catherine stood at the door in her reverie, the years following the birth of their first child seemed to have flown by. They were busy, happy years. Some of her memories brought a smile to her lips.

Ellen and Catherine counted themselves blessed. Their children flourished, and although they worked long, hard hours, they enjoyed the times they could attend the céilís and dances, which were arranged whenever possible. Whole families would set out on these occasions, and the children would play in the yards while the babies slept side by side on the beds. When the parents were exhausted from dancing the night through, children, babies, blankets and the dishes that bore whatever contribution they had made would be collected, and the little groups would reverse their journey, tired but refreshed. Patrick had quickly learned the dances and enjoyed the competitiveness of the other men – to be the best and most graceful on the floor.

When the bad times came, as they come to everyone, Ellen and Catherine were a comfort to each other.

One year there was an outbreak of erysipelas among the children of Killybegs. The work of the women was increased many times over. Laundry and clothing had to be washed constantly to slow the spread of the disease. Children had to be isolated and fed separately. It was a difficult time, and when the disease began to abate everyone was exhausted. But they felt fortunate, as none of the little ones had died.

Although the progress of the disease was halted, Ellen's oldest girl Mary still suffered from vestiges of the illness. Both Ellen and Catherine were surprised at this since Mary of all the children had until now seemed impervious to the many ailments to which the other children were prone. The fever and chills had left her, but a rash was ravaging her face, most particularly her eyes and vision.

The doctor had come and gone many times but was not able to add anything to the regimen he had prescribed. Mary was very frightened, and George was beside himself with worry. This was the daughter born after four sons, and he loved her past reckoning. He would sit with her and tell her of the activities about the farm and village. For a little while this would ease her panic, but Mary's increasing loss of vision would quickly send her into panic again.

In desperation Ellen went to sit with Catherine. After talking for awhile, Catherine said, "Ellen, I have oranges growing mold. Let me try to help Mary's eyes." Ellen knew that Catherine had a store of ancient lore passed to her by her father. Most often Catherine never used or spoke of any of it, and because of this Ellen realized that Catherine now thought there was no longer any alternative but this measure. She also knew that the oranges represented many hours of skilled handiwork bartered for the fruit. Ellen bowed her head for awhile and then looking up, she nodded.

While Ellen sat patiently, Catherine retrieved the oranges from where she had hidden them. The children craved the fruit, and although she hated to keep it from them, it was expensive and difficult to obtain. If she was able to barter for some she invariably kept it for medicinal purposes. Knowing how anxious Ellen was, she proceeded to prepare the unguent as her father had instructed her. When it was ready she gave it to Ellen with instructions.

Shortly after Ellen started to treat Mary's eyes with Catherine's remedy, Lent began. This was a very busy time at Leiter because traditionally the house was one of the "stations" visited by the priest of the parish during Lent. Mass was offered, and all who attended were given breakfast, as they had fasted overnight so as to receive communion.

The custom grew out of the use of large, isolated farmhouses during the suppression to offer Mass by priests "on the run." The practice in those years was extremely dangerous for those involved, and it was necessary then to have men watching for any movement of soldiers toward the farm where Mass was being offered. To be caught offering

Mass or carrying any of the sacred vessels meant certain death for the priest and, at the least, deportation and loss of property for the family and attendees. Leiter was ideal because of its location overlooking the surrounding country. There was a natural depression in the hillside behind the house; a large flat rock there was used as an altar. When necessary, the Mass vessels and smaller altar stone were hidden in a cave elsewhere on the property.

This Lenten time there was no suppression of the church, but an order against "congregating" was broad enough to cover any situation deemed undesirable by the military. Ellen's older sons made a game of it by going into town together; they were four in all, each over six foot and built to size. They were frequently accused of "congregating" but so far had escaped with warnings. Ellen worried constantly but opted just the same to host the Mass for the sake of the old people in the area who were unable to make their way to the church; they counted on "stations" such as hers to receive the sacraments.

She was determined to make the day memorable – particularly this year, when the service would be in memory of Canon Sweeney, who was sorely missed. He had died as he lived, quietly and with dignity. Ellen's comfort was that he passed while still useful and beloved by his parishioners – he had dreaded being parceled off to some home run by one or another order of nuns dedicated to the care of the aged and dying, there to wait until death mercifully claimed him.

All week before the appointed day Ellen, George and every available hand were busy cleaning, tidying, cooking and arranging. On the morning of the occasion the house and yard were spotless. Ellen regretted that her beautiful roses were not yet in bloom, but it was too early in the season.

As the congregation started to drift in, George coaxed Mary to sit in the large kitchen where the Mass was to be said. There was room enough to accommodate the number of people expected, but Mary was ashamed of her face and eyes and reluctant to be seen. With her father's persuasion she picked a dark corner and sat quietly, hoping not to be noticed. Her hopes were short-lived, however, since the room was soon filled by flocks of old women.

Immediately she was surrounded and questioned about her condition. Through blurred and weeping eyes she looked from one of them to another, trying to answer all their questions. Having extracted every bit of information Mary could offer, they gathered, their silvery white hair foaming above the black barriers of their shawls. Helpless to escape and unable to reach her parents, who were busy greeting and seating arrivals, Mary sat and awaited their verdict.

Whispering and contradicting each other, they reached an agreement. They turned to Mary with their decision. The leader of the group, a despotic beldame with her years etched on her face, said to Mary, "The timing is in the providence of God. If you will do as we tell you there is no question that your sight will be saved. Come now and follow us."

With that she was pushed ahead of them up to the center of the room and immediately in front of the makeshift altar. Having positioned her to their satisfaction, the spokeswoman said, "You are to kneel right here during the Mass. Don't worry lass, we'll be right beside. What you are to do is wait until the priest raises the host at the consecration and then creep forward to reach the hem of his robe. Press it to your eyes, asthore, and ask the good God to restore your health and sight."

Mary looked at them with horror. The fear of God, the priest, and her parents if she were to do such a blasphemous act left her without words. The old women saw this and quickly, each with their own version, began to relate precedents from the bible when many people approached Jesus and were healed by touching his garments. They pointed out that the priest was God's anointed one, and that the consecration was the holiest part of the Mass. Mary heard none of this rationalization but was overwhelmed by their insistence, by her respect for the old ones – which her parents demanded – and by fear of their anger if she were not to do as instructed. She was sure she would be more in danger from their displeasure than from God's wrath.

She took her place as instructed. The women gathered about her and watched while some of the younger, sharp-eyed men and boys were instructed to remain outside and warn of any unwelcome visitors. The priest entered in his robes, and the Mass began.

There was a warm, good feeling during the service – it was, after all, a celebration among friends and loved ones. Mary knelt, lulled into a sense of peace that disappeared when she was propelled into action as the altar boys rang the bells at the consecration. Several of the old women pushed her in turns toward the priest with loud whispers to "get on with it asthore, hurry, hurry." Desperately she reached for the vestment and pressed it to her eyes as the priest raised the host. Many years later she could still recall the cool, soothing sensation of the soft old linen.

Overcome with embarrassment, she shuffled back to her place to the accompaniment of sighs of satisfaction from her looming elders. She hardly heard the end of the Mass in anticipation of anger from the priest, her parents and the people gathered.

To her never-ending surprise the priest merely turned at the final blessing and offered her a special blessing. Several people patted her and said, "Good for you, lass."

By the end of the week the rash had nearly disappeared, and her eyes were improving rapidly. George was elated, Catherine was quietly pleased, the old women were convinced of their brilliance, and Ellen was grateful for the blessings of God.

§ § §

When the children were growing, Catherine and Ellen would take every opportunity to visit each other – not easily done with all the work of small children and the farm. In addition, Catherine continued to sew whenever the work came her way. One day when there was a brief pause from the unremitting demands on her time, she went trudging up the hill with the least child in her arms. As she walked, she saw Ellen's father Peter ahead of her. He had become a self-styled expert on raising children since he was now the doting grandfather of both Ellen's and Peter Og's bairns. He also felt that his newfound leisure, since his son had taken over most of the burden of the farm, had given him great insight into the proper way to run things.

This particular day he was on his way to advise Ellen on a remedy he had heard for a teething baby and also to give George his opinion of some cattle recently purchased. Catherine could see George with Con coming out of the barn. Ellen was in her garden tending to the roses she loved so well. Toddling behind Ellen was her littlest one, and waddling further behind was Ellen's pet goose. Catherine laughed to see them and paused to observe, for she knew what was about to happen.

Con and George halted as they came out of the barn. "Do ye know, George, I think I'll have my dinner from that goose one day. It's the divil's own creation and sure to God I don't know how you put up with it."

"Well, Con, I have to say I'm not fond of the bird, but Ellen dotes on it and the wee ones love it. If it's ever allowed in the house though, that will be the end of it. The boys are all terrified of the blasted thing — it surely hates men and boys, but it does keep the gossoons away from Ellen's garden. Do you think Peter sees the creature? For that matter, has he ever run into the bird?"

"Now that you mention it," Con replied, "I think the last few times he was here Ellen was busy in the house, and on those occasions the creature stays by its nest. Oh boys, let's watch the show!"

Ellen did not see her father approaching, but her pet did, and with feathers puffing and wings flapping the bird waddled over to him to begin her offensive. Peter impatiently waved his walking stick at the bird, shooing at it. Taking umbrage at this strange man invading her territory, the goose flew at Peter, hissing and attacking with its beak. Surprised, Peter stepped back to hit with his stick but the bird — a veteran of these encounters — was quicker.

Dashing at Peter's ankles she nipped at him until the old fellow was dancing with pain. Peter recovered his balance and parried the goose with his stick. The bird was adept and evaded his thrusts and stabs, flying over and under the stick until Peter with a snarl of rage grasped the cane with both hands and slashed at the goose.

Ellen ran to pull the little one out of range of the combatants and then turned to see her pet lying stricken on the ground. She ran toward them with cries of dismay. To her father's amazement, she turned on him saying, "Now look what you've done." She picked up the goose to assess the damage and turned toward the barn.

Peter sputtered loudly at this remark. "Is that all you've got to say after that imp of Satan attacked me, your own father?" When Ellen continued toward the barn he picked up his hat, which had fallen during the fray, and in high dudgeon strode off down the lane, not noticing Catherine who, doubled with laughter, was attempting to be invisible.

George and Con meanwhile were also convulsed with laughter. When Con recovered his breath he wheezed out to George, "Do you know, that bird has merit after all," at which they both began to laugh again.

Catherine had by this time reached Ellen. She patted the goose and reached out to stroke its head. The bird honked a pitiful welcome to Catherine and laid its head on Ellen's shoulder. The little group continued then toward the barn, Ellen leading, with the toddler behind carrying feathers, the spoils of the war. As they passed the two men, the bird stretched out its long neck and with pure malevolence in its eye nipped Con on the ear. He let out an oath which caused Ellen to remonstrate, "For shame, mind the baby's ears."

George was by this time wiping tears from his eyes. God knows, he thought to himself, that bird was a divil, but the show this afternoon was worth it all.

§ § §

Busy as she always was with the house, her sewing, and helping the neighbors, and grateful for Patrick's love and Ellen's friendship, Catherine would sometimes compare her life to that of the sister-in-law she had never met. Although she and Patrick had six children, there were no children born to his brother Thomas. They heard that the young wife spent most of her time hunting, and there were rumors that Thomas was drinking heavily.

Then one day Father Kilcoyne, assigned to the village following the death of the canon, came to the farm to tell Patrick that Thomas had been killed in a hunting accident. The news caused Patrick a double heartache. He had never quarreled with his brother and indeed had hoped for awhile that they could remain in touch. He was aware, however, that Thomas was totally governed by his mother and so was not surprised that his brother made no effort to contact him. Now he had not only lost a brother, he did not expect to be allowed to mourn for him with his family.

Father Kilcoyne stayed a long time with Patrick but could offer little comfort. The priest did express the hope that the Reverend Hamilton would do what he could to mend the breach.

Whether the reverend even spoke with his parents, Patrick never knew. He attended the funeral services for Thomas in the beautiful little chapel, but as usual his parents ignored his presence. Since they did not speak to him, he did not speak to any and left immediately after the service. He heard later from his cousin Kent that the wife had returned to her own people after expressing her unhappiness with the marriage and her in-laws. She never contacted them again.

Not many months after Thomas's death, Patrick's cousin

came to tell him that his mother was quite ill and not expected to live. Patrick with some bitterness asked if he would be allowed to see his mother before she died.

Embarrassed and upset, Kent shook his head and said, "Patrick, you know how I feel about this. Time and time again I've tried to make them see reason, to no avail. You would think after the tragedy of Thomas's death they would be anxious for a reconciliation, but they are both adamant. I'm sorry, Patrick."

"Oh Kent, I know you have stood a good friend to me and I can find no fault in your efforts. But for the life of me I cannot understand their position. Other neighbors and friends of theirs have had much worse happen in their families, yet the families stay together. How many black sheep have been shipped off to America and return home as heroes? Perhaps Catherine and I were wrong to stay in Ireland, but I love this country and Catherine did not want to emigrate. In any event, thank you for coming to tell me. When you see my father, please tell him he has my prayers and best wishes. There is nothing more for me to say."

The news of his mother's death came shortly after his cousin's visit. Catherine shooed the children out of the cottage and sat with her arms about him. The bitterness against Patrick violated every standard by which Catherine lived. She was not able to understand a woman who could die with her pride and arrogance clutched to her bosom. For herself she was indifferent to Patrick's parents, and it would not have disturbed her if they received Patrick and not herself, but she was filled with fury for the grief they had caused her husband over the years.

The sadness and depression stayed with Patrick for many

weeks, but eventually he shook the blackness of his mood and became his usual social self. He was well liked by the villagers, even though they tended to be formal with him. He was courteous and gallant with the women and because of this was frequently sought out for a bit of conversation. He was fond of a little gossip and would often walk down to the main road in pursuit of the latest news from the village.

Patrick recovered from his mother's death, but that year was uneasy and strange. News of rioting in Dublin, with many deaths, was followed by the announcement that the Protestant Ulster Volunteers were mobilizing to resist any attempt to impose Home Rule. This caused a great deal of consternation in the northernmost counties.

Then one afternoon in the early fall, the village was aroused by the shouts of children racing through the lanes, calling everyone to come to Fintra to see the fish. At first they were ignored in the belief that it was a childish prank or an occurrence of no interest to adults. But some of the older children made themselves heard, and soon groups of people carrying creels and baskets hurried toward the strand.

The day was unusually bright, sunny and warm. Because of this, the excursion took on a holiday air. The break in the daily grinding routine was welcome, and the women especially were pleased to be out walking, gossiping, laughing and free for a little while from the burden of loneliness.

The first adults to reach the beach were astonished by what they saw; they stood hesitating at the end of the road until they were pushed forward by those behind. Children danced in excitement as they watched the gleaming waves of fish hurtling themselves against the shore. Piles of fish, some dead and some still writhing, lined the water's edge.

Initially pleased by this unexpected bounty the families began filling their baskets with fish. It wasn't often that dinner lay on the ground waiting to be picked up. There was much laughter and good humor as they went about harvesting the gift. As the afternoon wore on and the light began to fade, however, the people grew quiet. Their baskets were full and still the fish kept coming. The children by now had become bored with this phenomenon and had returned to the village in pursuit of each other. Their parents stood on the hill slightly removed from the shore and watched as fish continued their frenzied effort to dash themselves against the land. The last rays of the sun reflected on the silvery scales, and rainbows of color danced on the water as fish leaped into the air, twisting and plunging toward death.

The old women had taken out their beads and were alternately crossing themselves and muttering the rosary.

Finally, exhausted by the sheer waste and senselessness of the orgy of death, the stream of villagers started back to their homes, quiet, subdued and awed by the spectacle. Some of the men returned later to see if the surge had ended. The fish were still teeming and racing to the shore. The water offshore was silvered by moonlight on the crest of the waves, and the fish had now become slashes of bright metal disturbing the calm evening.

By daybreak the frenzy had ceased, but for months after the old ones would cross themselves and speak of portents.

Immediately after that the village was stricken by an epidemic flu that was debilitating and difficult to overcome. Catherine and Patrick's youngest daughter Rebecca was one of the first to catch it. Never strong, she could muster no defense and was soon in the grip of consumption. Her parents were frantic. Catherine with Ellen at her side tried every remedy of which they had any knowledge. The doctor shook his head. What she needed was a warm climate, rest and comfort. Patrick in desperation sent a note to his father, to which he received no reply. And then began the long vigil.

On the nights that Patrick could no longer bear his daughter's torments he would walk the lanes until he was exhausted to the point of sleep. Catherine had no escape. She parceled the children out to Ellen and various friends and neighbors, but she remained constantly by her young one, desperately trying to relieve her suffering. Ellen would come and sit with her, but there was no surcease for mother or daughter.

When the end came it was a relief for all. Death was no stranger to the village, but Rebecca was a young and lovely girl, very popular with her classmates, and the pet of the family. Her death cast a pall over Killybegs, which added to the existing unease.

Racked with grief, Catherine cursed the man who would not spare a few pounds for his granddaughter. Patrick had no response to this tirade. His bitterness was immeasurable, and only the knowledge that it would bring further grief to his family kept him from assaulting his own father.

§ § §

And when it appeared that Patrick was regaining some peace of mind, there came new anxiety to deal with. Why God, thought Catherine to herself, do you test the faith of your people with such persistence? Having woken one morning to bustle about the hearth and start the morning meal, Catherine looked out the little window to see Captain

Kent riding up the lane. Although she liked the man, she had come to associate him with more trouble. Nevertheless, she put on a smile and hurried to the door.

He entered the room and by his presence caused it to shrink in size. Patrick was as tall as his cousin but had a gracefulness which made him blend into his surroundings; Kent had all the force and some of the bluster of many men with military training. He sat by the fire and thankfully accepted the tea Catherine brought him. Looking at him, she could see his face was white with exhaustion.

"You'll want to speak with Patrick. He's having a rest, but I'm sure he heard you. Bide a minute and I'll see."

Shortly after, Patrick came in to sit by the fire, still rubbing the sleep from his eyes. "Well Kent, what is it now. Can there possibly be anything else my father can think up to cause more pain?"

Obviously upset, Kent averted his eyes, drew a long breath and said in a low voice, "Yes, Patrick, there is."

Catherine wrapped her hands in her apron to stop their trembling and stood staring at Patrick, who was watching his cousin while anger stiffened every bone of his body.

"I was sent for yesterday because your father had an attack and was not expected to live. I have to tell you, Patrick, he died early this morning." Patrick made no response. So Kent, after a moment, went on.

"As you know, I am trustee of his will. I've discussed his decisions with him many times, Patrick, but was never able to persuade him to include you in it. I'm sorry."

"Ah, Kent, you are not telling me anything I do not already know. Forget it, man. There was not nor is there anything you could do. Have another cup with me and a bite

140

to eat."

"No Patrick, listen to me. You forgot the entail."

Catherine looked from one to the other. She knew Patrick was furious, but she also sensed that Kent was trying to salvage something for his cousin. Not having any knowledge of the legalities of the situation, she could only sit and wait for enlightenment.

Watching Patrick, Kent expanded on the legal position.

"Your father left all his money and most of his property to some cousins on his side. There is nothing to be done there. But despite the fact that he also left the house and surrounding property to them, it is not legal because of the entail. You can claim them as yours because you are the only surviving male heir, but you must do it immediately, before the house is occupied. If you go today and live in the house and light the hearth for twenty-four hours, you will fulfill the old Irish law and the English courts will honor the entail. Traditionally they deny any attempt to break an entail lest they set a precedent.

"I know you do not have the money to support the property at this time, Patrick, but it is very valuable, and I could help until you can turn some profit from farming or selling off some of the land — don't reject the idea until you've thought about it. Please Patrick, use your head."

There was still no response from Patrick. Then suddenly he bolted from his chair, grabbed his coat from a peg by the door and with no goodbye, strode out.

Catherine and Kent sat staring at each other. Finally he said, "Well Catherine — will he do it?"

"I haven't a notion. He has been sorely used through this entire time, and I know he has no fond memories of his home or family."

"I realize that Catherine, but this is a question of money. Wouldn't you be better off living in that lovely house with a chance that someday you could be a lady of leisure?"

"God love you Kent. I wouldn't know how to be a lady of leisure. As for Patrick, difficult as it is to understand, money is not that important to him. He wishes life could be easier for me, and Lord knows he would have done anything to save Rebecca, but it's too late for that now."

With that she bent her head and began to weep. After a moment she recovered and looked up at Kent, who waited.

She continued, "If the old man had the kindness to mention Patrick in the will or acknowledge the entail, perhaps Patrick would not be so stricken. But the mean and spiteful way he arranged the matter was meant to give more pain."

Silently he acknowledged the truth of this and to himself wondered what could have caused the parents to be so uncaring and cruel toward the son, who as far as Kent could determine was worth two of his brother. Perhaps it was only the fact that Patrick would not be led against his will. But it was exactly that — his strength of character — that made him such a fine man. It was a mystery that would not be solved.

Kent put down his cup, preparing to leave. "I can't add any more to what I've told you, and I must be on my way. There are many things to be done, but I will return later to hear what Patrick has decided."

And so it was. Catherine stood by the door watching for Patrick, who remained absent the whole day. She hadn't a notion where he'd gone and was concerned that he was wet, cold and hungry. She leaned her head against the doorframe and closed her eyes for a minute, exhausted and fearful of the effect this latest news would have on Patrick.

She was almost asleep on her feet when she heard the slow, dragging steps of weariness approach the cottage. She threw her shawl around her and ran down to open the gate. The fog was almost impenetrable, but she knew it was Patrick and she was almost shaking with anxiety.

When he reached the gate, she pulled him toward the house, crooning to him and urging him forward. As soon as they entered the bright kitchen, she sat him by the fire and kneeling, pulled off his wet, soaking boots. Taking his hands she began to chafe them, trying to bring some life to his eyes.

He suddenly grabbed her hands and almost violently said to her, "You must listen to me. God forgive me for any hurt I may do you, but they would not allow me in their house while they were living, and I will not enter it now they are dead. Do you understand?"

"Oh, Patrick, what do I care. We have what we need and that is enough. Their money never brought any joy to them, and God knows, aside from Rebecca we have been happy. Think no more of it, acushla, but come nearer the fire and warm yourself. I have the kettle on and you'll soon have some tea and supper."

She wrapped her arms about him and stroked his wet hair, rocking and crooning until his trembling stopped.

Patrick's refusal to occupy the house divided the village into two camps and was the principal topic of conversation for several weeks. The women, discussing the matter over tea, almost all agreed that they would take a broom to their man if he turned down such a wonderful opportunity. The men, however, while they sucked their pipes and nursed their pints, nodded and muttered that a man must be a man. It caused many a battle between husband and wife when the subject was discussed in the privacy of the home.

# VII

And then the increasing likelihood of war between Germany and England caused a tightening of security in the town. A curfew was imposed because of the vulnerability of the fleet at anchor.

Soon other events became more interesting to the villagers. Two of Ellen and George's sons left home. The story was that they were off to Scotland for work, but there were those who said they had gone into the hills.

Ellen was visibly saddened but brushed off any questions by saying that she missed their rowdiness, as indeed she did. She loved to dance, and Paddy and John would often come to her while she was working at the hearth and, picking her up, would spin their mother around the floor, telling her she was still the best dancer and the prettiest woman in all of Ireland. Often the other boys would join in the fun, grabbing Mary or one of the young ones for a spin around the kitchen. Oh indeed, she missed them.

But the missing was not the hardest part. When she went to her bed at night after telling her beads for the safety of all in the home, particularly for her two darling sons gone to fight what some called a fool's battle, then her courage deserted her, and she would weep quietly into her pillow.

George would pat her shoulder and say she shouldn't worry. Weren't they the clever lads and well able to care for themselves? But she would lie in the dark and think of their life in the hills with nameless, faceless men dedicated to a free Ireland. Poorly equipped, they would make forays against better-armed, -fed and -housed English troops.

She wondered where they lay their heads at night. Were they warm? Did they eat? Were they wounded? Although she would not voice her feelings, she often thought she would rather have her sons well and safe than have a free Ireland.

After the long sleepless nights she would rise in the morning to another day and put on a cheerful face for George and the children, particularly Mary, who sorely missed her beloved Johnny and Paddy. Always and always however, she warned the children to say nothing to anyone about their brothers. They had gone to Scotland looking for work, and that was that.

Paddy and John were not gone long when Peter came to the house early one morning. He was obviously upset and cocked his head toward the children still finishing their breakfast. George stared at him for a moment and then directed Mary to take the little ones into the yard and mind them for a bit. At the cries of dismay for their unfinished breakfast, Ellen told them they could take the food with them and shooed them out. She instructed Mary to check that they were neat and tidy after their breakfast and to send them on their way. If they didn't hurry with their breakfast, they would be late for Mr. McNealy's school. He would be angry, and Ellen wanted to be sure that her children got the worth of the penny she was paying for their lessons. She turned then to listen to her husband and father.

"What is it Peter? What brings you here so early?"

"By my faith, George, I think we're in for it now unless we can work something out."

Over the years George had accustomed himself to old Peter's love of the dramatic, and he knew that patience would be rewarded with the information he sought, but there was a quality to Peter's distress which caused him to believe that this time was indeed serious. Besides, he thought to himself, he wasn't getting any younger and had less and less time to cater to Peter's fits and starts.

"Out with it then, man. Sure if it's that serious it needs immediate attention. Here, take a seat by the fire. Ellen, bring your father a cup of tea. Now then, what is it."

"Well," said Peter, tamping at his pipe and arranging his cane and legs comfortably as George rolled his eyes in exasperation, "You know there has been a lot of activity among the boys because of the war and the departure of some of the garrison. Be that as it may, there was a shipment of arms dropped on the beach during the night. The shipment was expected, and most of the bands showed up to claim their share of the contraband. But there must have been a warning of some activity in the area because the way from Mountcharles was cordoned off, and no one from that area was able to get through to pick up their guns.

"God knows there are plenty willing to sell information; one of the layabouts in town must have hoped to collect a shilling or two for the information that there was a shipment of guns being dropped."

George interrupted him. "What now makes you think it's a layabout? I am afraid they may have a bigger problem in Mountcharles. None of the men in the movement are stupid enough to mention an arms shipment in a tavern or any other place, so who is leaking information?"

Peter was a bit stunned by this version of the situation. He chewed on his pipe, mulling over the unwelcome thought that the leak might be closer to home. But then chivvied by George, he proceeded with his narration.

"Anyway, the fishing boat that dropped the arms hung offshore for most of the night and was preparing to return and recover the remaining guns, but the coastal patrol was seen coming about the head, so they set off for open waters. As yet, no ground patrol has come by that section.

"The patrol boat has been at sea for a few days and probably did not know the warning of an arms delivery. It's possible the captain of the patrol boat thought the fishing boat was a poacher, but he is sure to report an unknown vessel, and then there will be a reconnaissance sent to check the area. The hiding spot is deserted and not easy to reach, so that gives us a wee bit of time.

"If the guns are found on the beach, everyone in the village will be questioned and harassed until someone gives up the information the English are looking for. Aye, we will be lucky if many of the young men are not picked up on some trumped-up charge. There will be harassment even if the guns remain hidden, but it will only be from suspicion. Without the guns, the situation should settle down quickly."

George sat very still for awhile. "I won't ask how you know all this, for it is more than I wish to know, but tell me: Where can the guns be hidden? Every house will be searched if there is even a thought that guns are about."

Looking up from under his eyebrows to assess the reaction he would get, Peter replied, "They must go by cart

148

to Mountcharles. Once past the checkpoints that have been established and before reaching the village, the cart will veer off unto a lay-by and the lads will be waiting to move them. Then the cart will proceed to my granddaughter's cottage. She's expecting her first, and Tessa is there with her now."

"What then do you want? I do not have the breath to help you move and load guns. Paddy and John are away, Jim lives in Mountcharles with his wife, Michael's away with the fishing boats, and I won't let Eddie help you — this house is watched since Paddy and John have gone. They would pick Eddie up right away; the less he knows, the better."

"No, no, it is not the moving and loading of guns that is a problem. Some lads from the other bands returned knowing there was a cordon about Mountcharles and that those boys could not go through to pick up their share. No, no, the guns have been moved from the beach," Peter said.

And then with a glance from under his eyebrows at his daughter and an intake of breath he announced, "I have them now, here with me, in the cart."

George leaped from his chair, bringing on a fit of wheezing and coughing. As he struggled for breath, Ellen rounded on her father in a fury.

"What do you mean bringing those guns here. What about the children? God help us all if the English know you have them."

"Hush, hush, lass. There are those who are watching out. No patrol has left the garrison yet. As I said, since the fishing boat was laying well out to sea and there was no activity to be seen ashore, the captain probably included it in his routine report as poaching, but that only buys us a little time. There is only one beach in that area, and it will be searched. If there is even the slightest sign of any activity the hunt will be on, but as I said it will only be a suspicion."

"So now you must tell me, and tell me quickly, what is it you want from me?" demanded George.

"I need Mary."

"Are you daft, man? Do you think I would let her go with you in this mad scheme even if I knew what help she could be? Get away with you. You're dreaming."

"Listen, listen, George, it's not as daft as you think. It's been well thought out."

"Who thinks my daughter is a pawn to be tossed into this lunatic scheme?"

"Ah sure I can't answer that. It's not for me to say. But let me tell you the plan.

"I am plainly an old man, and the drive to Mountcharles is more than I would normally undertake by myself. Taking a young lad with me to help would surely cause the wagon to be searched. If Mary were to share the driving — and we know she can manage the team — we would have a good chance of being passed through if we can go quickly before there is any alarm raised.

"Listen, man dear, this is not a thing I would ask if it were just meself to think about, but there will be the divil and all his minions to pay if we don't get these guns away from here."

Ellen stood shaking her head in refusal, but George sat pondering the problem and knew that what Peter said was true: If the English tipped to the fact that there had been a shipment of guns, they would not rest until someone paid. The fact that Peter had brought the wagon to Leiter would be reported. There had to be a reason for him to have done so, and the guns had to be moved. To keep them here would be suicidal.

Reluctantly he nodded and staved off Ellen's anguished cries, saying, "There is no choice. It must be done.

"Now then, Peter, if we are to do this, let's do it properly. Firstly, who knows that you are attempting this mad jaunt? I will not risk my daughter without some assurance that her role is a secret. And secondly, what is your reason for taking the cart to Mountcharles?"

"The only one who knows of this attempt is himself, whom I will not name. He bound me to tell you that while he is aware there has already been a breach of security, there cannot be another in your case, for only he and I have discussed this plan.

"It is my thought, George, to get a load of peat from you. It's well known that you have the largest bog in the area, and it would not be remarked if I came to you for a load since I have very little left from the last cut and have not yet started on a new batch. All in the village know that Tessa has been called to Mountcharles because her daughter is not well and the baby is expected early. They will be needing to keep the fires up even though it is still quite warm."

Ellen burst in saying, "Let me go with you. It's known that I'm a midwife — it won't be questioned."

"No, no, Ellen," Peter replied. "You have not delivered a baby ever in that area, and isn't your son Jim's wife the district nurse and on call if needed? No no, simple is better. The child would think nothing of being pressed to help with all the lads in the field for harvest and myself too old to make the journey alone. Her face will not give her away, for she knows nothing.

"There is something I would ask you to do, though. If you could do it quickly, would you pad and cover the wagon seat? Just a rough job with some nails. Then we'll be off."

Ellen hurried to get some old sheepskins. George raised his eyebrows at Peter and said, "Aren't the guns in the seat?"

"Oh aye, but I'll have a few tricks up my sleeve."

George went to the door to call Mary and left Peter giving instructions to Ellen as to his requirements. Ellen also thought it prudent to send some baby clothes and food. It would be the normal thing to do, and the packages could sit atop the peat, well wrapped but available for inspection.

Mary was thrilled at the chance to travel to Mountcharles with her grandfather. Any break in the routine of her days was welcome, and she was chuffed to think that she would be chosen to help in the home of her cousin.

She was ready in minutes and came out of the house to see that the cart had already been filled with the peat and Ellen's contributions. Her grandfather was sitting comfortably atop the sheepskins that his daughter had quickly tacked to the box seat. Although she was surprised that her grandfather was prepared to leave so quickly – most days he would be content to sit and drive both Ellen and George to distraction with his advice – she assumed that he was wary of Tessa's tongue if he failed to deliver the peat in good time. She climbed into the wagon, marveling at the comfort of the sheepskin padding, and turned to bid goodbye to her parents.

To her surprise, her mother's face was twisted up and she seemed almost in tears.

"Don't worry, I'll take care of grandda and try to help aunt Tessa. Everything will be all right." Her father came to her and gave her a warm hug. Oh my, she thought to herself, everyone is so strange today. Maybe the birth is not expected to go well.

At that, Peter gave a loud crack with the whip, and the cart started off down the road.

Going down from Leiter required all her grandfather's attention, and he said nothing until they reached the main road to the north. He turned then and began to tease her about all her beaus. Since Mary had been and still was known to be almost as wild and daring as any of her brothers, these remarks were a surprise to her, but not unwelcome. She was, after all, sixteen and had recently noticed that some of the lads were trying to catch her eye. She waved her hand at her grandfather in denial but was secretly very pleased.

As they turned the bend into the road to Mountcharles they saw a young garda leaning against his bicycle. He was checking the wagons but obviously had had little traffic that morning, since he was busy whittling a piece of wood.

He was a local lad who had joined the Royal Ulster Constabulary like his father before him. Village opinion ran two ways about the R.U.C.: Some felt it a necessary evil and preferred the numbers to be composed of local men, while others thought anyone joining was a traitor to Ireland. In the case of the young garda, judgment was suspended since he and his father made every effort to bridge the gap between conflicting interests as fairly as was humanly possible.

Because of the ambivalence of his position, he was not always privy to the reasons for certain orders, so presently he was not particularly anxious with respect to current orders to search all wagons traveling the road.

He looked up and was pleased to see Peter. All in the area knew that Peter had not only opinions about everything, but also the desire to express them, most often with wit and creativity. This would pass the garda's time.

Peter hailed him as they approached and called, "What are ye up to, young Dorian. Have ye nothing better to do than sit in the middle of the road?"

"Surely to God, I'm pleased to see you. I'm supposed to be checking for contraband, but neither contraband nor any other thing I've seen since I got here. And I see you've got your lovely Mary with you."

Mary blushed and turned away from his admiring looks. He tried one or two other remarks, but she was not equipped to banter with him; she was confused and shy about this new attention.

To her relief, he turned to her grandfather. The young man looked quickly into the wagon and asked Peter, "And where are you going with such a load of turf and this the summertime?"

"Oh well, you know how the women are," said Peter. "My oldest granddaughter is expecting her first. It seems to be an early birth, according to the women, and they have it in their heads that the fire will need to be kept up if the wee baby is very small — 'tis true I suppose that the nights do cool down. Tessa, my daughter, said that the granddaughter's turf from last year is almost gone, so I had my orders to go to Ellen's and get some. George always has more than they use with that big bog on his land. My darling Mary is riding with me to help with the drive and give Tessa a hand if needed."

"Sure then I hope everything goes well for the little one.

But tell me, what sort of a rig is this you've got over the box seat? You know, don't you, that I'm to check every wagon."

"Oh aye, and there's a tale in that which is why the bits and pieces that Ellen is sending to Tessa are sitting atop the peat," Peter said.

With that he pulled his pipe and tobacco pouch from a pocket and leisurely began to fill the pipe to his exacting requirements. When this was done, he struck a match on the side of the wagon, applied it to the tobacco and began to puff thoughtfully at the pipe.

The garda looked at him with expectation. He knew from experience that Peter would not be rushed with his stories, but the morning had whiled away in such boredom and with so little traffic that he was glad for the company.

Peter now seemed to have the pipe burning to his satisfaction. Turning his attention to young Dorian again he said, "It's my arse, you know."

Dorian ducked his head to hide his laughter and, peering from under his lashes, looked to see Mary's face blooming bright scarlet. Man dear, he thought, this will be good fun.

Peter puffed for awhile on the pipe, nodding his head and thinking.

"Do ye see," he said. "It's like this. When I was a wee, small lad, the only concern I had was for me belly and how I could fill it, and me legs and how fast they could carry me — especially when I was trying to get out of a bit of work. In my youth I still had a care for filling me belly, but me legs lost pride of place to me rod and ballocks. And only myself knows now how much trouble they gave me. They led me a chase all over the county. I had many a frolic and many a close escape from an angry da or sweetheart, but I wouldn't have traded a minute of it. No sir, no sir, I would do the same if I were to do it all over again." With that he gave a great sigh and fell to musing silently on his young days and the thrill of seduction.

Mary knew there was nowhere for her to escape. She sat rigid on the seat, avoiding the side glances of the young man – and vowing never again to go anywhere with her grandda.

Her grandfather roused himself from his reverie and proceeded. "When I met my Mary Dugan, my wandering ended, for my desire was toward her and never anyone else again." And gazing fondly at his granddaughter he said, "And isn't my darling here the image of her beautiful grandmother and the apple of me eye. Ah, wouldn't my Mary have been proud to see this lass."

He brushed his hand to his eye and continued.

"It was me back and brawn then that got my attention. I needed all my strength and more for the wife and children. 'Twas easy getting them but hard raising them, as many a man has discovered then and now.

"But the years passed and as I got older me stomach demanded attention. I suppose the abuse it took over the years and grief for my loss caused it to rebel against my habits, but that passed with care.

"Now in my old age the humiliating truth is that I have to worry all the time about this old arse of mine – where to sit it, and is there a proper cushion. Do you not think it's very undignified for a man to be as careful of his arse as a young woman is with the bottom of her first-born child?"

Dorian was obviously dumbstruck by Peter's own presentation of the ages of man, and as he struggled to think of a way to drag the situation back to the matter at hand, he saw coming 'round the curve two wagons following each other closely.

He cursed quietly to himself. There had been no traffic at all on the road until now, and his orders were to search each wagon, but if he were to hold Peter's wagon long enough to search the box seat, the other wagons would back up, causing a roadblock. And roadblocks were situations detested by the men of the hills. Dorian didn't suspect the backup was deliberate, while both of the oncoming drivers were young men — namely the two McVeigh brothers — and the potential for trouble was far greater with them than from Peter and his granddaughter.

He made his decision. Sending the lead wagon on its way, he lightly admonished Peter to remove the sheepskins from the seat before long, saying that not every checkpoint would be as easy as he was. He smiled broadly, winked at Mary, who had been wishing she could disappear, and turned his attention to the other wagons.

As he did so he could hear Mary expostulating, "Grandda, how could you say such things. What will he think of me?"

Peter turned to his granddaughter in surprise saying, "Why would he think badly of you, child? Sure you said nothing a'tall."

With that he clucked at the horses and snapped the whip to hasten them on their way. When they were well past the checkpoint, he put his pipe in his pocket and chuckled.

They were good men, the McVeighs. They could be counted on to do as asked and not a question from them. He wondered what load they had invented to take to Mountcharles this morning.

It was a good thing they came when they did. He knew that very soon young Dorian would have demanded that he open the box. Now if all went well, that would be the only checkpoint. He hoped to be in Mountcharles before there was any alarm from the patrol boat. He was tired. This was no game for an old man. With a drained look on his face, he turned to Mary and asked her to take the reins for a bit.

Mary knew as she looked at him that her grandfather was more tired than he would ever admit. Her mother would skin her if anything happened to the grandfather while she was supposed to be easing the journey for him. Mary took the reins and asked her grandfather if he wouldn't feel better lying in the back of the wagon. She offered to spread out a bit of blanket for him to rest.

Peter was sorely tempted by the offer, but since he was not easy in his mind, he shook his head in refusal. He feared another checkpoint. If they were lucky, the soldiers would not yet be organized. But he felt he had to keep his wits about him; if he were to be sleeping when they came upon a patrol, he would be at a severe disadvantage. He patted Mary on the arm to relieve her anxiety and said he was not that tired and just needed a few minutes to revive himself.

They continued quietly on their way. Occasionally Mary would glance at Peter to see how he was, and as a half hour or so passed the color seemed to return to his face. He also seemed to have become more cheerful and began humming some lively tunes to himself.

As they traveled further and further, Peter became more hopeful that they were past any danger. Just as he was thinking they were safe, a patrol of soldiers preceded by an officer lounging in a motor car driven by his batman came down the road, drew up about a quarter mile ahead of them and proceeded to set up barricades.

Peter's heart lurched. For himself he had no fear — at best his years were very short — but he loved the granddaughter who was so like his own Mary, and he cursed himself for bringing her into this danger. But he remained convinced they had not had any choice.

Not turning his head, he told her quietly to slow the horse as gently as she could and let the animal amble at his own pace. Then, turning his back in order that Mary could not see, he took a great wad of tobacco from his pouch and chewed it until he was able to swallow it. Getting the mess down was difficult, and as they neared the soldiers he could feel the nausea rising in his gullet. He began to sweat.

The officer in charge was bored. Protecting the empire against a raggle-tailed bunch of hoodlums was certainly not what he had trained for. He was near the end of this assignment, and he was ambitious for a more interesting post. This furor over some fishing boat was not his cup of tea, but the natives were going to pay for disturbing his morning. His batman opened the car door and he got out, yawning and stretching as he did so. By this time the little cart with Mary and Peter was fairly close, and he became conscious of the pretty young girl. Now then, he thought to himself, I wouldn't mind detaining her for a bit. He strolled over to supervise the search.

Two of his men had deployed themselves to either side of the cart. But before they began to question the pair, the officer took over.

"What is your business on this road today?"

Mary turned to her grandfather, but Peter was obviously

in some distress. Looking from one man to the other in confusion she blurted, "We're on our way to my cousin's house. She's expecting her first and my aunt Tessa sent for some peat. The baby is expected to be very tiny and they're fearful it might not live without the warmth of a fire."

With an expression of distaste, the officer said in an aside to his men, "Just what we need. One more crazy Fenian in this world." Turning to Mary, he asked, "And hasn't a pretty girl like you got better things to do than drive with your grandfather? I'm sure if you looked about you there are many possibilities."

This pleasantry earned him a blank look from Mary, who was not certain what he meant. Realizing that he was dealing with a country girl who could not or would not banter with him, he barked at Peter, "And why is your seat covered with that unsightly sheepskin. Don't you know we have to search your wagon?"

Peter was by this time terribly ill and sweating from the effects of the tobacco. Mary put her arm about him and glaring at the officer said, "Can't you see he's an old man. My mother put that padding there to make the drive more comfortable for him. I would have come by myself, but he did not want me to be on the road alone, and all the men are out harvesting. And it is a very fine skin. One of our best. He's not well, can't you see that."

Pleased at the show of spirit from one he thought stupid, the officer reached to pat her cheek. Peter growled as Mary recoiled in embarrassment and terror. The officer, smarting at her rejection, instructed Peter to get down from the wagon — they must search it.

Peter, holding tightly to Mary so she could not jump

from the wagon, made some shifting moves as a preliminary to climbing down. As he did so the tobacco that he had been struggling to hold down spewed up from his throat and unto the wagon and Mary, spattering the officer's boots as well.

The officer jumped back from the wagon shouting imprecations at Peter and every living Irishman.

"Get these dirty peasants out of here. What are they doing holding up traffic? Look at that backup! Have you men no sense? Move this abominable wagon. Get it out of here! Where is my batman? I curse the day I saw Ireland."

Mary, mortified by the incident and terrified that the officer might change his mind, snapped the whip at the horse and urged him to his top speed.

Young Dorian's inspection of the McVeigh brothers had been cursory after he checked their wagon seats, enabling the brothers to follow closely behind Peter and Mary. Having then driven their teams as fast as possible to stay close behind Peter, the McVeigh brothers now quickly pulled into the space to await search and distract the soldiers.

The quantity of odds and ends they had managed to pile into the wagons on the pretext of helping a friend move his household would ensure that the patrol would be kept busy for a good while. Meanwhile the officer, in a fury at having seemed a fool in front of his men, was berating the unfortunate batman who was attempting to clean his boots. Mary and Peter departed unnoticed.

"Ah Mary dear, I am sorry for having messed you. We can't stop now to clean up, for I'm anxious to be away from here as quickly as possible. Can you bear with it for awhile, my dear?"

"Grandda, grandda, I'm worried about you. You look

something awful. Will I stop at one of the cottages and get some help? There's a little place up the road, I'll stop there."

"No, no, don't stop. Do as I say, child."

Unwilling to disobey him, Mary kept the horse trotting at a good pace. Her attention was divided between the road and her grandfather, so it wasn't until she was nearly upon him that she saw a man jump from the roadside bushes. He grasped the horse's bridle and pulled the wagon off the road. She turned in fright to her grandfather, but he calmly bade her get down from the wagon and wait there, back from the road where she would not be seen until he returned.

The wagon with the man and her grandfather in it jolted away over the field. Stunned and uncertain, Mary sat. And then conscious of the unpleasant condition of her dress, she went to the little brook at the roadside and tidied herself.

When the wagon arrived at an old barn, unused and decrepit, the man jumped down and several others came from the barn to help him with the unloading.

The leader of the group approached saying, "Peter, Peter, is that the stench of the English you have on you? What happened, man dear?"

"Oh, as God is my judge, lads, I was sure my days were numbered. After the first checkpoint was passed with no trouble, I thought we were in the clear. But thank God my little trick worked, and wasn't it a good thing the wee lordling was more concerned with his boots than with contraband."

His face suffused with anger when he added, "I wanted to do murder when he reached to touch young Mary." Shaking his head, Peter stopped for breath.

The man who had waylaid the wagon continued the

story, telling them of the checkpoint and Peter's ploy to evade a search. They looked at Peter with respect. Any of them would have done the same, but it was the quickness of his thinking that impressed them.

It was obvious that the trip had taken a toll on Peter, so one of the younger men took him into the barn, helped him to clean up and provided him with a cup of tea. He sipped at it gratefully but insisted that he must leave as soon as they unloaded. He was afraid for Mary and wanted her safely at her cousin's home. She knew nothing, but the road seemed to be well patrolled and he did not want to chance someone remarking that it took an unusually long time to go from the checkpoint to the cottage — some time could be accounted for by their effort to clean themselves up.

Since this made good sense, there was no more discussion and the same man who had stopped the wagon went ahead to scout the road and make sure Peter and Mary did not blunder into a patrol or, for that matter, a traveler whose curiosity would be aroused by such an unconventional appearance from the thicket.

When they arrived at the little cottage, they were greeted by Tessa in a rare frame of mind with worry for her daughter and a newly arrived grandson. With barely a thank you for the peat she said to Mary, "Build up a steady fire in the hearth and keep it burning. We will need quantities of hot water for laundry. Set as many kettles as you can to boil, and I wouldn't mind a cup of tea for myself."

Mindful of her mother's instructions to be useful, Mary started on these tasks. But first she looked into the basket her mother had sent. There she found a crock of buttermilk, a great slab of butter, freshly baked bread and cold potatoes which had been mashed with cabbage. Worried about her grandfather, she poured him a glass of cool buttermilk, settled him comfortably by the small fire and said to him, "Drink the milk, grandda, and I'll fix a little dinner for you as soon as I do what Aunt Tessa needs me to do. My mother sent food, and it just needs to be heated." Exhausted and half-dazed by the experience, he patted her arm and laid his head back on the chair.

Mary thought he looked poorly. She didn't think she could get her aunt Tessa's attention for her grandfather just yet. Perhaps later when the baby and her cousin were settled.

Sometime later Tessa emerged from the room behind the fireplace with a tiny bundle in her arms. She placed it in the cradle near the fire and bade Mary call her if the wee baby made the least noise. Mary set her foot on the rocker and kept up the gentle motion of the cradle, as she had seen her mother do many times. Tessa, assured that Mary was capable, returned to the backroom to confer with the doctor and district nurse. There was still concern for her daughter.

Unsure where to direct her attention, Mary sat between the baby and her grandfather, turning from one to the other.

After a little while, her grandda seemed to revive a little and said to her, "Mind you lass, there is no need to mention our little detour on the road. Your aunt Tessa is upset enough, and your father knows I was to see some old friends on the way. We'll just keep it as our secret. Do you understand, Mary?" Taking her nod as agreement, he put his head back in the chair again and slept.

They did not return to Leiter for a few days. Tessa needed Mary to help and was also concerned at Peter's appearance. She said to him, "What have you been doing old man? You look like the backside of the barn. Couldn't you have found someone younger to make the trip here?"

"Go away out of there. Where would I find someone with them all out in the fields with never enough help. Don't worry, I just need a wee rest." He knew that this was Tessa's way of expressing concern, and he was content to remain for a day or so. Mary was elated with her new position of responsibility and the novelty of being away from home. She was content to stay.

The checkpoints remained in place for several days. The village was uneasy, and every move in or out of the barracks was noted and discussed. The patrols were sent out randomly and frequently — with no results.

The garrison commander was heard to roar in frustration, demanding to know "where the bloody guns could have gone." Because of the fishing boat and the traces of activity on the beach, the commander was convinced that the guns had come ashore. He believed they could not have passed the checkpoints, and in view of the number of men and hours it would require to transport them by foot, the commander also believed the guns were still in the area. He called in the senior sergeant-major to review the situation.

The sergeant stepped briskly into the commander's office, snapped a salute and braced to attention with his chin tucked into his neck and his shoulders impossibly rigid.

"Sergeant. You are aware, I presume, of the seriousness of this matter."

"Aye, sir."

"Well then, are you able to explain to me why we have had no results? You have had carte blanche in the number and size of patrols to be mounted, you know it is imperative that the guns do not reach the outlying towns. They would be dispersed into that godforsaken mountainous, treeless country to the north, and every croppie farmer and son would consider it a pleasure to shoot an approaching patrol. You know it is almost impossible to govern that area. It is too exposed. Why have we not recovered these damned guns?"

The sergeant stiffened his already rigid back and ventured to say, "Sir, my men have been patrolling all areas at every hour of the day and night. They have observed no movement. The weight of the guns would indicate that they were moved by wagon. It would take at least a half dozen or more men to move thirty or forty guns, which is what we're estimating. The guns could not have been moved by foot."

The sergeant's opinion was met with frigid silence. The implication that the guns could have been smuggled past the checkpoints could only reflect badly on the officer in charge of the checkpoints, and the commander was of the opinion that the sergeant had overstepped his position — it was not a sergeant's place to question the efficacy of the officer responsible for the search.

With a chill in his voice the commander asked, "Do you have any grounds on which to fault the stringency of the checkpoints?"

"No sir, no sir. Perhaps the guns are still in the area," the sergeant replied.

Whatever suspicions the sergeant may have had, he was not prepared to voice them. He knew that to pursue his suspicions would embarrass the officer, which ultimately would be detrimental to his own career. Standing at attention, he was instructed to search any likely cottages and buildings using his own good judgment. He was also instructed that he need not be too careful in his search. It was the commander's thought that "these people need a lesson." The soldier saluted and, swiveling on his heels, left the office. He knew exactly where he intended to start his search. He had his informants.

Mary and Peter arrived at Leiter the morning after the soldiers had come. When Peter saw the condition of the yard, the turf hurled about, the vegetable garden trampled over and his daughter weeping over the ruins of her beloved roses, he thanked God they had not returned the day before. A lovely young girl at the mercy of the loutish soldiers might have given them more information than she realized. She knew very little, but enough to have put the English in the right direction.

Ellen, tears streaming down her face, warned them that the house was destroyed. The soldiers had come during the night and roused them from their beds. They had questioned George and Eddie. They were very rough, and Ellen feared for her husband. He had taken to his bed unable to breathe, but the doctor had come and gone, and George appeared to be more comfortable. Eddie, bruised and cut, was out in the barn working. Ellen told Mary to go into her father. He would rest easier knowing she was home safely.

When Mary entered the house, she burst into tears. The floorboards were torn up and all the furniture was strewn about. Smashed china and feathers covered the exposed earthen floors. The feathers rose and settled with each gust of wind through the broken windows. Her mother's lovely, ordered hearth was a mass of dented and broken pots and pans. The religious pictures that adorned the kitchen were trodden underfoot amidst the bits of small, cherished ornaments. She turned to go up the stairs until she realized that they had been ripped up. She saw then that her father was propped in a contrived bed in a corner of the kitchen.

His head was down and his hands were clasped in prayer, but at the sight of his daughter he smiled broadly and holding out his hands said to her, "Don't worry, asthore. We've all survived, and the rest can be replaced. You must cheer your mother and help her to tidy. Thomas will come with some of the men to restore the floors, but they are waiting until the soldiers have stopped searching. We were not the only house they ransacked. I think, however, that we bore the brunt of their anger. It seems they were looking for guns, and since your brothers have gone to Scotland, they are suspected of joining the rebels."

This was as much as he felt was wise to tell her, and after patting her on her shoulder and assuring her that he was fine, he asked her to send Peter in to see him.

"Oh, and Mary," he added. "Talk to Eddie. Try to calm him. He was beaten and swears he will not stay to be treated this way in his own country. You know, asthore, I'm not well, and your mother will need him. Go to him and see that he rests. As you can see I've been no help this day, and he is trying to do it all himself. That's a good girl. And tell your grandfather I need to see him."

Mary went out. When she stopped to speak to Ellen and Peter, her mother took her by the hand, saying "Mary dear, you look as pale as a ghost. Don't worry, child of mine, nothing has been done that can't be mended. Give Eddie a hand for a little while. Just do what is necessary and then come into the kitchen. I'll have something hot for you and Eddie. Go on there, and try to smile."

In truth, though she would not say as much to her mother, it was not the damage that worried Mary so much but the words of her father. It was unlike him to admit to ill health, and to say that her mother would be needing Eddie was, she thought, a way of warning her that he did not expect to live much longer.

The fact of his age was something she had always tried to ignore. Until now, he had always been active and in full charge of the farm.

Mary was devastated. The relationship between her and her father was special. Her mother never understood Mary's need to be doing something physical – riding, dancing, running to town on errands, chasing stray sheep with the dogs – anything, as long as it didn't entail being quiet. Her father never objected and always said to Ellen, "Let the child go. She can't sit still."

And at the day's end, they would talk for hours about the farm or the news from his ever-present *London Times*.

Oh God, she couldn't bear it if he were to die.

Determined for her father's sake to relieve her brother's depression, Mary went into the barn.

§§§

One morning not many days after Mary and her grandfather returned, her uncle Thomas came slowly up the road. As Ellen watched him approach, she knew by his posture and pace what he had come to say. Taking her by the hand, he led her into the kitchen where George was sitting by the hearth.

"It was a very easy death. He died in his sleep. I went looking for him this morning when he wasn't by the fire making the tea. He was always the first one up. Och Ellen, he could drive me wild but as God is my witness, I will miss him terribly."

George nodded to himself. He knew that the trick with the tobacco had been too much for Peter's old heart. He loved the man despite all his shenanigans, and although it was not a story to be told, he had died for his granddaughter and his country. Peter would be proud of that epitaph.

George held out his hands to Ellen. She took his but continued to stare blankly at the fire. Peter was an old man, but he was her bond to both her deceased mother and her own childhood. He was wonderful company and the best gossip in the town. The death of her father seemed to foreshadow the death of her own husband. They were close in years, and George had been ill for a good while.

§ § §

In the autumn the fishing fleet returned from the Atlantic. It was doubtful they would be able to go to sea again while the war continued. From there on the men who counted on fishing for their living were anxious and restless. Sunday's sermons were frequently addressed to those men who tried to drown their frustrations in drink.

Ellen knew that her son Michael was a frequenter of the public house, but she felt there was more to it than the loss of the income from fishing. There was plenty to support him and his wife and child if he decided to work on the farm.

Although neither she nor George had approved of Michael's marriage, they had accepted the girl. To do otherwise would have driven Michael away.

The girl he married had lived in town with her parents,

but they were newcomers by local standards. Her parents had come to Killybegs before her birth, and the father set himself up as a blacksmith. There was enough work to keep him busy, and the townspeople appreciated his convenience.

Try as they could, the local gossips could find out very little about their background. Stories went about that the woman was a tinker. Her appearance seemed to bear this out: Although she was quiet, well spoken and reserved, her posture and carriage bespoke a freedom of movement foreign to the women in the village.

As the daughter grew to womanhood, the rumors were resurrected again. The girl was beautiful, with a sensuous quality and wild beyond anything seen in the village before. She was the center of any gathering of young people and the cause of many fist fights among the young men. She seemed to enjoy pitting one against the other. When it became clear that her parents could not, would not control her, the parents of the other young girls began to forbid them to associate with her.

To Ellen and George's consternation and Michael's pride, the girl settled her favors on Michael. He was tall, handsome and a marvelous dancer; half the girls in the town were hoping to marry him. She became pregnant, and the wedding took place. During her pregnancy and for awhile after it appeared that she was content with her life.

But during the summer months while Michael was away on the boats, Ellen heard stories that her daughter-in-law was restless. Since she had almost no contact with the girl and no proof, she tried not to judge her. Any effort on Ellen's part to get close was met with a rebuff. Determined to let the young couple work out the problem themselves, she said nothing to Michael when he returned.

Others did not have her restraint.

Michael had been home only a few weeks when he came to Leiter one evening. Standing awkwardly by the fire, he told his mother and father that he had come to say goodbye.

Neither of his parents were able to speak for awhile. Finally George asked him, "What do you mean, 'you're leaving'? Don't you have a wife and child to provide for? Are they going with you? Where in God's name are you going? Where will you find work? Don't you know there is work and plenty on the farm? You have only to say the word."

Belligerently Michael answered, "I don't think my wife gives a tinker's dam where I go." He laughed bitterly as he said this. "I am not staying here to play the fool."

Mumbling, he told them, "I have heard stories since I came in from the fishing. I asked herself about the tales, and she did not deny them. She asked what was she to do when I was away long months at sea. I told her I could work on the farm, but she'll have none of that. Says she does not want old crocks looking over her shoulder."

There was not much to add. It was plain to Ellen and George that Michael felt his manhood had been destroyed.

Desperately searching for words to ease his hurt, Ellen said, "The fault does not lie with you. Your wife is what she was born to be; there is nothing you can do to change her.

"'Tis the nature of the woman to be flighty. Bring the child to us and stay and work the farm. If you give her a bit of money from time to time, she will be content. I think she has little liking for the bonds of matrimony."

Nothing they said mattered. He would not stay and wear horns. When finally he rose to take his leave he told them,

"She says she will care for the boy if I send money. The English are recruiting in the town, so I'm off to join an Irish regiment. My pay, or most of it, will go to the wife."

Having said that he turned to his mother, and blinking to hold back his tears asked, "I know you didn't want me to marry, and I should have listened, but the child is mine and I would like to know that he is cared for. Would you see to him every now and then to make sure he is not neglected? She seems fond of him, but if he becomes a hindrance to her good times, I'm not sure what will happen."

With despair in their hearts, George and Ellen rose to bid him goodbye. Urging him to stay would be useless. They knew his pride and the blow it had received. Wrapping her arms about him, Ellen kissed him and said, "God bless you and keep you. Go safely and return again to Ireland." Michael turned quickly and hurried out the door.

Michael had not been gone long when there came a soft knocking at the door one night after all had gone to their beds. Ellen, whose ears were always tuned for the summons to someone's need, rose to see who was there. As she pulled it open, the door fell upon her with the weight of the man leaning against it. Without thought her arms reached to embrace the man who was sliding to the floor. She knew immediately it was her son Johnny.

In the shadows of the yard she saw several men, but not their faces — the men from the hills took great care to remain anonymous. What was unknown could not be told. A disembodied voice whispered, "We're sorry for the trouble we bring you ma'am. He's not well and there was little we could do for him. And ma'am, oh jaysus..." his voice broke, and Ellen could hear soft murmuring and rustling.

Again the voice floated across the yard. "Your son Paddy, he ... it couldn't be helped. We were not able to bring him home to you. He fell in an action and ... we could not recover his body. We're sorry for your troubles."

They disappeared into the night. Holding the weight of her son in her arms, all she could hear was the moaning of wind hitting the shore after its journey across the Atlantic.

She held John closely to her breast and felt him burning against her. His eyes were closed and he was not conscious of where he was. He lay against her, helpless. She called to George, who had wakened at the knock, and between them they were able to half drag, half carry him to the little room behind the hearth. With tears running down her face and hands shaking, she examined him. She put her ear to his chest and listened in despair to his labored, shallow breathing. His pulse was very rapid and weak. He had pneumonia, she was sure. The months of living and sleeping in the cold dampness of the mountains with no creature comforts had exhausted him. God knows what could be done for him in this extreme state, but she would try.

Leaving George to prop up their son, she climbed to rouse Mary without disturbing younger sisters Lena and Sally sleeping in the room with her. When Mary was awake enough to understand, Ellen instructed her to build up the fire and set the water to boil for steam. Pulling some blankets from Mary's bed she went into Eddie's room, and shaking him from his adolescent slumber, she helped him pull on warm clothes. He was to go for the priest. Ellen was well aware that all her skills would probably not reverse the devastation wreaked upon her son.

She ran back down the stairs and entered the little room

where Johnny was lying. She looked at George and saw grief etching new lines in his well worn face. Their eyes met and acknowledged the futility of their efforts, but try they would.

Without words they worked, tuned by many years of companioned labor to anticipate what was necessary – but to no avail. As they watched in anguish their son slipped further and further away. Mary sat silently in a corner waiting for new instructions and praying for her beloved brother. At her mother's instructions she had already arranged a table with linens and candles for the priest to administer the last rites of the church.

Breathless and anxious, Eddie returned with the priest. Ellen met them at the door, but they did not speak, for the priest was carrying the host. Leading the way with flickering, darting candles, Ellen brought him to her son. The priest looked at Ellen and George and knew by the sorrow in their eyes and the small shake of Ellen's head that it was useless. With a sigh he prepared to anoint the boy.

George went to rouse his two youngest daughters and their brother Joseph. He returned, gently pushed them into the room, and placed them kneeling in the corner, fearful and crying. Mary and Eddie knelt, pressing closely to each other. Mary held her youngest sister Lena in her arms, while Eddie tried to comfort the others by holding their hands. Ellen and George slid to their knees by the side of the bed. They knelt shoulder to shoulder, Ellen clutching the limp hand of her son while George patted his foot. The candles dappled the walls with light until a gust of wind would cause the crouching darkness to leap from the corners of the room. The children cowered together knowing there was no comfort to be had from their parents.

At the words "te absolvo," tears began to stream down Ellen's face. "What," she thought bitterly, "is he to be absolved of. Being a boy with a boy's hope for a place in his own land? For not listening when we told him he was on a fool's errand? And weren't he and Paddy the best of sons. Were there ever two such willing, cheerful workers and good to us all. Wurra, wurra, who would raise sons in this country with no future. And I'll never know where Paddy is buried. I think my heart is broken."

With his free hand George grasped Ellen's, and in the wavering candlelight, to the priest's chant, they watched the life drain from their beloved son. As the first rays of the morning sun lit up the small room, dimming the brilliance of the candles, Johnny regained consciousness, but only to smile at his mother and father and whisper to them, "I'll be on my way now. Don't worry."

A pall settled over the house. Mary couldn't believe that her beloved Paddy and Johnny were dead. Where was the music, the dancing, the singing that they always brought with them? Gone, all gone. Her father tried to comfort her, but he was manifestly not well, and this only increased her sorrow. Ellen was locked into a silent grief that was impenetrable. The best and the bravest were gone. The two brothers had been inseparable in life and continued so in death. But life went on.

The routine of the farm forced a form of sanity on their grief, and the days passed. Just as it seemed that they could learn to live with their grief, the priest came trudging up the hill to the farm. Reluctance was pulling at his heels, and he could barely look at Ellen as she came to the gate to greet him. He took her hand and drew her into the house, where he knew he would find George. Although they almost knew

176

what he was about to say, the faint hope to which they hung stopped their questions.

With pity in his eyes, the priest cleared his throat and said, "There is no way to tell you this but straight out. The telegram came to his wife this morning. Michael is missing and presumed dead. His regiment was thrown into the thick of the fighting. They were raw, untrained young men and the casualties are horrible.

"Many in Killybegs have received telegrams. Some of the families will be in desperate shape because their young lads joined to bring some money into the house, and now they are dead and gone, God help us. I know it is no comfort to you to know that others are suffering, but we will have services for all the families together as soon as I can make the arrangements.

"Tell me if there is anything I can do for you; if not, I must be on my way. It will be very late when I have finished all my calls, and I wish to God I had more to offer than additional sorrows. I must see if I can get some relief for the families who are destitute. God bless this house. I will call back again. You are in my prayers."

Blank incomprehension augmented the sorrow that lay over the house and family. Mary felt detached from everything around her. Voices were distant, and she would stare in confusion when forced to concentrate on what was being said to her. Her mother was unapproachable, and her father was visibly retreating from life. There seemed to be no hope. Each day had to be gotten through. Each night they prayed for sleep.

Mary knew that long after the house was quiet and all were presumed to be sleeping, her mother still sat by the fire saying her rosary beads around and around. Many nights she rose from her bed to sit with her mother and respond to the sorrowful mysteries. There were nights when Mary was not sure her mother was aware of her presence, but she stayed with her in an attempt to give comfort.

Mary's father seemed to be in less need of comfort. It was Ellen he worried about. It was terrible enough to lose three sons, but she had bathed and prepared the body of only one. He knew how she longed to have held the others for even a little while. She did not even know where they were buried ... their graves were lost to her forever. His sorrow was to see her burdened by such grief and then add to it with his own death — for he knew he would die soon.

At the first blast of the cold winter, George took a heavy cold, and his overworked lungs could not sustain the new burden. Ellen sat long hours with him, holding his hand. There was nothing else to be done. Mary would relieve her, but soon the tears would start to flow and Ellen would return to sit by his side.

They had said all there was to say to each other, and Ellen never stopped loving the man who had created a whole new world for her. She knew he had held to life as long as he could for her sake, but the sorrow of losing his sons had been too much. He no longer had the desire to rise in the morning and struggle for breath through the day. It would be a mercy for him to go. She knew this, but it did not ease her pain. Barely able to speak, he would pat her hand and repeat, "Ellen, Ellen, my dear."

Ellen was almost glad when George stopped breathing. She could no longer bear to watch him suffer.

Once more they followed a coffin to its resting place.

Once more the neighbors gathered in respect and love for the family. And when it was all over, once more the family tried to gather up the bits and pieces of their lives.

It seemed as if the very fabric of their existence had been torn, never to be restored. The strength that Ellen had always shown deserted her. Try as she would, she could not rouse her interest to Mary's physical decline, nor the fact that Eddie was working himself to death trying to maintain the farm. The young boy Joe would try to help, but as yet he did not have the physical strength to match. Ellen knew they needed to hire someone — by this time of year George would have made arrangements for help on the farm. But she seemed unable to make any decision.

The other children were spending time with Tessa when they could be spared from chores. Ellen didn't care. She had lost a father, a husband and three sons. Her world was destroyed. Neighbors came and went, as did the priest, but there was no response beyond a detached politeness.

Catherine would come in the evening when she could escape her never-ending chores. She would bring a piece of handiwork with her and sit next to Ellen by the fire. At first Ellen would sit staring into the flames with her hands idle in her lap. More than anything her idleness wrenched Catherine's heart. She had never known Ellen to sit without occupation.

At first Catherine made no attempt to rouse Ellen, but after a week she pushed Ellen's basket toward her and asked, "What have you been working at? Is that a cloth you're stitching? I don't think I've seen it before. May I see it?"

With a startled look Ellen groped in the basket for a beautiful piece of table linen that needed last touches. She picked it up and began to embroider. Catherine breathed a silent prayer of thanks. Picking up her own work, she began to tell Ellen the news from the town.

# VIII

On a market day not long after, Ellen looked about her for one of the children to run an errand to town. As often happened these days, they were nowhere to be found, and she could not remember if they had said where they were going. Baffled, she tried to decide if she really needed the embroidery threads for which she intended to send someone. She sat staring at her hands and realized that if she could not employ them doing needlework in the evening, she would surely go mad. The fine work she did for extra money soothed her. Gathering her shawl and purse, she set out for the village. She had not been there since George's death.

After purchasing the thread and sundry other small items, she determined to visit her grandson, whom she had not seen since the funeral. Avoiding those who would pry and snoop in the name of sympathy, she walked swiftly toward her son Michael's cottage. Ahead of her she saw a woman trailing a very young toddler by the hand. As she got nearer Ellen saw that his face and clothing were dirty. She recognized her grandson and his mother and hurried to reach them. Before she did, a man approached them and held her daughter-in-law familiarly by the arm.

As he turned the woman toward himself, Ellen saw that she was well advanced in pregnancy. The child could not be

Michael's. Ellen started forward but caught herself, realizing that the village would love to talk of any confrontation on the road between Ellen and her daughter-in-law. Without speaking to anyone she hastened back to Leiter.

She paced the floor for what seemed an eternity before Mary returned from one of her rambling, lonely walks. With no explanation, Ellen instructed her to go to Michael's cottage and "tell that woman that Ellen Meehan will have her son's child. Tell her I said you were not to return without the boy and there is to be no discussion."

Looking at her mother's face, Mary knew better than to question her. But it crossed her mind that Ellen was more animated than she had been for many months. Although her face was pale and thin, there was some color to it and sparkle in her eyes. Shrugging her shoulders, she turned listlessly to do as she was told.

Arriving at the cottage, Mary knocked and waited. She could hear a man's harsh voice directed at a child, who was crying. The door opened and Mary's face turned bright red when she saw her sister-in-law's condition.

Seeing the expression on Mary's face, the woman laughed and asked, "And what is it you want, Miss Prim and Proper?" Pulling herself together Mary said, "My mother wants Michael's son. She said I'm to stay until I can bring him home with me." The door banged in her face.

Mary stood at the door debating what to do. Her mother had been quite clear in her instructions, and she did not want to return without the little one. When her mother gave orders in that tone, she meant to be obeyed.

With a sigh Mary decided to knock again. Just as she was about to do so, the door opened and the baby was thrust at her along with a poorly wrapped bundle of what seemed to be his clothes. The door again slammed shut.

Resigning herself to allowing the little lad to weep all over her blouse, she wrapped her arms about him and hurried home as quickly as she could. Her mother was waiting at the gate when she came up the hill. Ellen reached out her arms for Michael. He looked up at her and with a sigh nestled against her. Some of the ragged lines that had marked Ellen's face smoothed, and peace settled in her eyes.

The days after that saw great improvement in Ellen's behavior. With her grandson toddling after her, she bustled around asking questions about the farm and any requirements the boys had. She arranged for help in the fields and set the younger children to tasks that had been neglected because of her disinterest.

She also noticed that Mary had lost an alarming amount of weight and marched her off to the doctor. He advised that Mary be relieved of some of the more arduous jobs she had undertaken to help her brother, and that she get lots of fresh air, food and rest.

In an aside to her mother the doctor said, "You know my dear, she is a young girl and suffered much in a very short time. She needs to grieve and needs time to heal her sorrow. The work she is trying to do in order to help on the farm is really too much for her. I know she has been raised to farm work, but enough is enough. She is not a big, brawny lad. Ellen, if you don't give her permission to do nothing, she will continue to work herself to death."

Ellen was devastated that she had not noticed Mary's condition sooner and undertook her cure with a vengeance.

Although Mary was pleased to have her mother's

attention, she found the imposed inactivity difficult. On nice mornings, after Mary helped in the dairy and with the routine chores, Ellen would shoo her away, telling her to stay in the fresh air and be sure to get home for a good tea and milking time. Sometimes Mary would take Michael Og with her, but he was very young and not company for her. She took to wandering along the shore watching the boats and occasionally borrowing a rowboat to go out in the bay.

One sunny and unusually warm afternoon she was sitting on a rock by the shore skipping stones into the water. The sea was sighing and swelling with the promise of a storm, and the sullenness suited Mary's mood. Her feet were bare and her skirts were hiked up. There was no soul to be seen, and she had been wading in the water.

"May I join you?" The question seemed to come from nowhere. Leaping to her feet she whirled about, trying desperately to tidy her skirt in the process.

The lad facing her was about her own age, and he stood some distance away. He was dressed as a midshipman. Mary thought he must be from one of the warships waiting in the harbor for supplies and repairs. Baffled that he was even speaking with her, she slipped on her shoes and said she was just about to leave. Neither she nor any of her family or friends had any dealings with the English navy or military. There were some women in the village who "entertained," but Mary only knew of this from whispers exchanged among the young girls. Certainly none of her friends had ever been approached by a junior officer. She stood tentatively, knowing she could outrun him if necessary, but curious to know why he spoke to her.

"Oh, please don't go just yet. This is not the first time

I've seen you, and I've been trying to get my courage to the sticking point to talk to you.

"As a matter of fact, last summer I saw you quite often with two chaps. Sometimes you were on horseback with your hair streaming behind you like a valkyrie. That's a splendid horse and you ride bareback – how do you do that?"

Mary, unsure of the reference to a valkyrie and embarrassed by his obvious admiration, blushed slightly at the reference to the horse. Her father had been very keen on good horseflesh. His means of improving the breed would be questionable by English standards, but according to her father he was merely allowing nature to take its course.

She dodged the question and replied, "You must have seen me with my brother Eddie and his friend Packy. Last year was different. My father and older brothers were alive."

He started to ask about this but was prohibited by the expression on her face. Although he was stationed at sea and had little exposure to the "Irish Question," he was well aware of the tense situation between England and her colony. Unwilling to tear the tenuous threads of their rapport, he stopped himself and instead asked, "Do you live near here?"

She turned and pointed to the hill crowned by a white house that could be seen from where they were standing. "There, that's where I live with my mother, two brothers, two sisters and my wee nephew. It's called Leiter. It's a good farm."

"Oh I say that's jolly. Such a big family. I have an older brother, but I hardly know him. He was five years ahead of me and we were in different schools. He is the heir, and I am to make the navy my career. That's traditional in the family."

Mary was somewhat taken aback at the mention of heir

and tradition, but her curiosity was aroused, and she was amazed that he could say he didn't know his brother. She asked, "How is it you can say you don't know your own brother? What about the school holidays – don't you go about together? At Christmas and Easter and other family gatherings don't you have a good time with his friends and yours? Wouldn't your mother and father be angry to hear you say such a thing about your brother?"

Leslie, for this is how he introduced himself, laughed and said, "I don't think they would care. I hardly see them, for that matter. They travel a lot. At least they did before the war, and they are frequently in London for various reasons. And of course I was away at school as soon as I turned six."

"But who took care of you then? When you were sick or hurt, did your mother come? Didn't you get homesick at school? Did you want to stay there? Did you have a lot of friends? Wouldn't you rather have been at home?" Mary blurted out in astonishment.

"Old nanny has taken care of me since I was born, and if there was a problem during term the matron for the younger boys took care of it. When I was older, I reported to the infirmary. All the boys were sent from home at six, so there were chaps to play with. As far as wanting or not wanting to go away to school, there really isn't a choice. That's the way it's done."

Mary was relieved to hear that his granny had cared for him, and when he burst out laughing at her misconception, she became indignant and started to walk away. He ran to confront her and said, "I apologize for laughing, but if you knew my very elegant, remote grandmother you would see why I think it funny to picture her caring for a grubby little boy. No, the nanny I'm speaking of was my nurse and my brother's and father's nurse before that. I'm very fond of her.

"But please don't go away. You see, I really have no one to talk to. The other midshipmen use their time off to play cricket or rugby, and sometimes I want to be by myself. It gets dreadfully noisy and rackety, and after the closeness of the ship's quarters I just have to get away from them. They don't understand it and I take a fearful ragging, but all in all they leave me alone. I'd love to hear more about your brothers and sisters."

So, they commenced a friendship: the lonely English boy and the grief-stricken Irish girl. She loved to hear of the huge house and estate where he lived, while he was insistent on hearing the details of her life. At first she could not understand his interest in the little happenings of which her life was composed. As time went by, she realized that the events that seemed so ordinary to her were more foreign to him than his possessions were to her. The manifestation of ordinary human emotions such as love, affection, anger and sorrow had been denied him. To express any of them would not be acceptable to his class.

One day, in response to his question as to what she had for her breakfast, she replied casually, "stir-about." This remark elicited one of his peels of laughter. This no longer disturbed her since she realized that it was not derogatory.

"Mary, what is 'stir-about'?"

"Och, sure it's only oatmeal but we call it that because if it we don't stir it about it gets terrible lumpy and no one wants to eat it. My mother goes fairly mad when we won't eat what is put in front of us. Oatmeal is supposed to be very good for you."

Responses such as this made him very pensive. It revealed to him a lifestyle of accommodation, caring and warmth of which he had been unaware.

Mary by now knew that Leslie had little if any interchange with his parents and brother. He would love to visit with her family, but it was impossible. Although the caring for Michael Og had done much to ease Ellen's grief, her emotions were still raw from the terrible losses. If her mother knew of their meetings, Mary would be kept home. There was little cause for trust between the Irish and the English, and this odd friendship had to remain her secret.

The review of her life that occurred as a consequence of their friendship helped Mary to a new appreciation of the love which had and still did surround her. Leslie and she did not meet often because he was frequently at sea. But when his ship was in, Mary knew he would wait for her at their original meeting place.

As time passed Mary reminded herself often that there was no future with this lad. She kept the meetings on a friendly basis, but she could not deny to herself that she cared about Leslie.

When she first met him he was just a boy, but with each trip to sea he aged. The war wore on and the lines of stress in his face deepened. His eyes revealed what he refused to speak of. Instead he would begin to question her about the activities of her brothers and sisters. What did Eddie do on the farm? What were orphan lambs, and why did she and her sisters care to nurse them if it was so tedious? He was particularly fascinated by the doings of Michael Og, her nephew: the new things he learned, feeding himself, talking, helping his granny.

One day Mary said to him, "I'm thinking that my brothers are going to give Michael Og to the tinkers if he doesn't behave."

Curious, Leslie asked, "Why is that? I thought everyone was terribly fond of him?"

"Oh aye, and that they are, but the wee rascal has formed up a team with my mother's pet goose and is driving my brothers wild. You see the goose hates men and boys usually, but she adores Michael and follows him everywhere unless my mother is about. Whenever my brothers do something Michael doesn't like, he and the goose sneak up on the guilty party and the goose nips them. Then Michael runs as fast as his fat, wee legs will let him with the goose waddling after him honking as loud as can be. As I said, Eddie and Joe are furious, but my mother thinks it is funny."

Leslie laughed at this and said, "Oh Mary, your family is wonderful. You don't know what it is like to be alone at the mercy of servants. Many of them are kind and caring, but when all is said and done, they have their own lives to live."

Mary saved all the bits of gossip she could, knowing that when he was at sea, he reviewed them in his mind and kept the horrors of war at bay. Once in a conversation about what they would do when the war was over, Leslie asked "Mary, have you ever thought of emigrating to America or Canada, or perhaps Australia?"

At first Mary thought to treat the question lightly with a bit of song about leaving Ireland. But looking at him she realized that it was a serious question, so she said, "Oftentimes I've thought I would like to leave Ireland and all its troubles behind me. I have to think of my mother though. Neither of my sisters nor my brother are old enough to take over from my mother, and she will need my help for a few years yet. It's a big decision to make, but my cousins do well in America."

Leslie nodded, apparently satisfied with this answer, and they spoke no more about it that day.

§§§

One evening at the start of the third year of the war, Catherine came bustling into Ellen's kitchen, panting from the climb up the hill. Ellen told her to sit a minute and rest.

"Mary, put the kettle on. Catherine, you must take more care of yourself. Did you have to race up the hill?"

"I must tell you something," Catherine said.

Ellen turned to Mary, who was terrified that someone had seen her with Leslie. "Leave us for a minute, dear."

But Catherine shook her head. "No, let her stay. She will need to know sooner or later."

"Ellen, asthore, you know Patrick's cousin Kent has always kept in touch with him and has been a good friend through it all. He stood by Patrick and helped when he could. God bless him for that. Well, this day he came to tell Patrick news that is still secret." And then turning, "Mary dear, do you understand?"

"Oh yes, I would never tell a soul," Mary replied.

"Good then. He told my Patrick that there have been very heavy losses among the English and colonial troops in France and elsewhere, as you know, and that in order to man the front lines there will be widespread conscription. He is sure my son Packy will be picked up. The enlistments have fallen off and the English are desperate for men. Kent thinks that it will go very badly for young Patrick: Blaine is an

Anglo-Irish Protestant name. If he is assigned to an English battalion, he will be treated as a traitor when it is known that he is Catholic. If he goes to an Irish battalion, it might be worse since there are many here who have little reason to love the Blaines. Kent thinks Patrick must leave for America.

"I don't know whether I am coming or going. Patrick and I have talked it over and there seems no solution but for him to emigrate. But oh, Ellen alana, that is not all of it."

Catherine grasped Ellen's hands and with anguish in her eyes said, "You know that this means they will be after Eddie also. I don't know what to tell you asthore. The good God knows you have had enough sorrow, but if Eddie stays in Ireland he will be conscripted. Kent does not like the news he is hearing from the front — apparently raw troops are being sent in to fight, and Kent says it is nothing more than murder. You know this better than anyone."

Ellen's face turned ashen. If young Patrick was on the conscription list then it was almost certain Eddie was also. They were of an age and in their spare time were always together. The thought of losing another son — even if it were only to leave for America — was more than Ellen thought she could bear, but she knew that if his friend Patrick went, Eddie would want to leave with him. Eddie had been talking about America and his cousins. He was sure they would take him in and help him get settled in America. His restlessness was obvious. Ellen sat down heavily next to Catherine.

"When does Kent think the conscription will start?"

Catherine replied, "There is not much time. He wasn't sure, but there will be an offensive soon, he thinks, and they will want soldiers before then. For the front lines, he said."

"God help us is there no end to the troubles the English

bring. I know Eddie will never serve in an English army. Better he is gone before the matter comes up. I do not want to think of him in an English prison. Have you made plans?"

"Kent is quietly trying to find a list of American ships making the voyage back and forth," said Catherine. "He has to be careful because the news of the conscription is still secret, and he has no reason to be inquiring about ships to America. As soon as he hears something, he will let us know. He says a ship out of Londonderry would be best. It's much closer and my son would have time to travel there as soon as Kent hears of a ship. All the sailings are kept very secret, but if they are in Londonderry when the ship is loading, Kent thinks it would be easy enough to get passage. The Americans don't care about a conscription in Ireland."

Ellen sighed and said, "There's nothing for it but to send them both. Have you said anything to Patrick?"

"No," replied Catherine. "His father and I will speak to him this evening. I'll be back when I hear more. Think on it Ellen. I hate to be the bearer of more bad news for you, but God knows I had little choice."

After Catherine left, Ellen and Mary sat staring at each other. They both knew what emptiness there would be with another of the boys gone.

"It isn't fair," Mary blurted to her mother. "What do men care about the sorrow and loneliness left behind them? They go off without a care and we're left to worry and work." Then she saw the look on her mother's face. She remembered Johnny and Paddy. Well, she thought, they certainly paid for their dreams. They went to battle in their youth and pride. Where were they now who died before they ever lived. Eddie himself was just twenty. She began to cry.

192

"Enough of that now," Ellen said. "We have to think about the money he will need. I wish I could barter for his passage, but that's not possible. Tomorrow we'll go over his clothes and see what he will need.

"Oh, Mary asthore, don't you know it does no good to cry. We'll make the best of this, as we have all along. It has been very hard on you, but in this life it is a long road that doesn't turn. There is nothing more certain than change, and you can be sure these sorrows will pass. Be a good girl and try to keep a cheerful face. It helps."

Mary was never sure who her cheerful face helped, but cheerful she tried to be, and the bustle of preparation for Eddie's departure kept her too busy to think very often about how lonely she would be without Eddie and Patrick. Patrick had been at the farm so often she counted him as one of her brothers. They were two years older than she, and Mary had tagged after them since she could toddle. Until they started to chase the lassies, she had been with them on all their adventures. With them she had herded sheep, fostered the orphan lambs, and learned to ride and shoot. But they had also taught her dance steps and the latest American tunes, and lectured her on a lady's behavior. No one could fill their place in her heart.

Eddie was very pleased at the prospect of emigrating, especially since his lifelong friend would be with him. He and Patrick had often talked about America. It seemed to be the ambition of every young Irishman. There would be work and a chance to better themselves. 'Til now it had only been a dream for them – Eddie because he felt he was needed on the farm and did not want his mother to experience more grief, and Packy because he was reluctant to leave his friend and family. Patrick's mother and father still mourned the loss of Rebecca. His other two sisters had married and emigrated with their husbands. Any attempt he made to raise the question of emigration was met with tears from his mother and his father's comment that, "America has all the Irishmen it needs. Ireland needs some of her own."

Eddie and Packy regarded the conscription threat as a mixed blessing. To emigrate was their desire, but since they were sworn to secrecy over the proposed conscription, they were suffering guilt for the possible fate of friends they could not warn. Both Ellen and Patrick's parents repeatedly told them that it was not their secret to tell, and to do so would surely cause Kent to pay a penalty, if he was not imprisoned, for having revealed military information.

Because of the need for secrecy, there were none of the usual farewell parties or "American wakes." Packy and Eddie kept to their everyday routine, fretting that the conscription would begin before Kent heard of a ship willing to take them. Eddie had the additional worry of instructing his young brother in all the minutiae of the farm. He knew his mother was well able to run the farm now that she had shaken the torpor that threatened to overwhelm after his father's death, but Eddie was anxious to relieve her of as much of the burden as possible.

Finally the message came for them to leave immediately for Londonderry. An American ship was loading, and if they arrived in time they would be accepted as passengers.

With small packs containing all they could carry they departed early the following morning. Eddie had said his goodbyes at home, and his eyes filled with tears when he turned at the bend in the road and saw his mother's figure etched in black against the brightening sky. As he waved to her, she turned toward the house. By custom she would not watch until she could no longer see him — that might foretell his disappearance from her life.

§§§

Silence sat over the house after Eddie left. Ellen was trying to come to terms with the wreckage of her family. Out of six strapping sons and three daughters, she was alone with three girls and a son not yet sixteen to keep the farm going and support them all.

Michael Og was her salvation. Too young to know of the sorrow she had experienced, totally enchanted with his new life, and doted on by his young aunts and uncle, he darted about the farm and with his antics and smiles brought some joy to her life. His mother had made no attempt to regain him, and although Ellen was prepared to fight for him and would have the support of the village and the priest, she was relieved not to have the worry of it all. She had also heard that there was another wee baby boy born to her daughter-in-law. It was just as well Michael Og stayed with his granny. If his mother had neglected him before, it was certain that he would have been abandoned altogether in favor of the new baby.

Now that her mother seemed to be herself again and in control of the farm, Mary decided to work in the rug factory in town. Ellen was not happy with Mary's decision. She said, "Why do you want to go into the town and work all day sitting at a frame. Isn't there enough work and plenty to keep you occupied at home?"

Mary shrugged. While she knew she wanted some

money set aside for plans she and Leslie had been making, she could not say this to her mother. Instead she said, "Oh but you know any of the girls in the village who can are working at the rug-making. It'll be a bit of money I can put aside, and you know I'll meet some of my friends there."

Indeed, Ellen knew that many of the local girls worked there, some to help at home, some to save for marriage or emigration. Although the war still raged across Europe, the news that American troops had landed in France raised expectations that it would soon be over. Realizing that the return of the young men serving in France would mean the end of their employment, the girls worked long hours for extra wages, but they used their free time to spend the extra they earned. It was freedom such as they had never experienced. Money of their own – to spend as they wished.

The first day she went to the factory she was crossing the road to the building when she spotted her schoolgirl friend Annie. Mary ran and with a cry of delight grabbed Annie, who was jumping up and down with excitement.

With simultaneous cries of "I didn't know you were working here. When did you start? What do they have you doing?", the two girls were swept into the building with the crowd, all chattering and relating news of what had transpired since they saw each other two days ago.

While they waited to be assigned, they exchanged personal news. Annie was well aware of the deaths in Mary's family, but she wanted to know all about Mary's life since then. Promising to meet for their tea break, they were sent to different areas.

Over the next weeks Annie and Mary became privy to each other's secrets. Annie, who was the oldest of a large family living on a barely profitable farm, confided to Mary that her mum and da were allowing her to keep some of her earnings to make up a dot.

With happiness shining from her eyes, Annie said, "I'm promised to Aemon Brennan. Remember him, Mary? As soon as he returns from France we are to be married. I didn't want him to sign up, but he said it would be the quickest way to put aside some money. It can't be much longer, can it Mary, now that the Americans are in it?"

With a smile Mary said, "Ah sure it won't be any time a'tall. I remember Aemon well. You and himself were always thick as thieves, even though he was one of the older lads."

Blushing, Annie acknowledged that they had always had an eye for each other, and then she asked, "And what about yourself? Have you no fine bucko in mind?"

After swearing Annie to secrecy and threatening her with awful consequences if her secret were revealed, Mary said, "I met one of the English sailors. He's a midshipman." Seeing Annie's shocked expression, Mary hastened to say, "No, no, Annie. It's not like that. He's a perfect gentleman. We met accidentally. He was lonesome and weary of all the constant talk of war on or off the ship. It was just after my father's death, and it was wonderful to have someone to walk and talk with and not have them asking all sorts of questions that I didn't want to answer. Even though I'm afraid to tell my mother, he is nice and kind and not taking advantage of me. I have to say something to my mother soon though, because we've talked about emigrating.

"His family, I know, would never accept me, and he wants to be shed of all the rules and regulations he has lived with all his life. Leslie, that's his name, tells me he has a little money left to him by one of his grandmothers, and he thinks it will be more than enough to set ourselves up in Canada or Australia.

"Oh, Annie, I want to be away from all the troubles. Am I terrible? Do you think I should leave my mother?"

"Ah Mary dear, who am I to say what you should do. I would be terrible afraid to leave my family and Ireland. You know that is one reason why I love Aemon. He always protected me. You're different Mary. You were more often daring the boys than playing with the girls. You would love to set off for a new country and a new life. I know your mother, Mary; she would never hold you back. You should tell her something though. It's not fair otherwise."

"I will do that, Annie, but not yet. Telling everyone will take some of the joy out of it. There will be questions and lectures, trips to the priest, and everyone will be wanting to meet him. He's never dealt with anything like an Irish family before, and he might run away altogether."

Mary laughed when she said this but there was, she knew, some truth to the statement. She was banking on his need to have her emigrate with him. She knew he felt deeply for her, but the sheer size of her family, communal interest and intense Catholicism would be a deterrent. She also knew, through their conversations, that no girl of his own background would undertake the life he sought, fulfilling his own dreams away from the bonds of his family and class.

Mary craved reassurance, and she would wait until she saw Leslie again. He had promised he would have plans made when he returned from this voyage. That would be time enough to speak to her mother, and they would have a definite proposal to give her. Mary decided to put it out of her mind for now.

In the fashion of young girls eager for pleasure and company, Annie and Mary went to all the dances and parties to which they could walk or coax a ride. The days passed, and although each of them longed for the return of their beau, it did not dampen the sheer exuberance of their youth and beauty. Annie was as she always had been, timid and cautious, but she was content to go where Mary led, and Mary was pleased to have her as a companion.

One morning as Mary arrived at the factory and went to her place at the frame, she was surprised to have one of the older women approach her. The woman had a puzzled, worried look on her face.

She stopped Mary from situating herself and said, "Mary, Annie's little brother came to say that Annie would not be in today, and he asked would you be able to come to their cottage quickly. He ran away before I could get any more out of him, and I'm sure I don't know what can be the matter. Do you mind, Mary? If you get back quickly I'll see you don't lose your pay. It's very worried I am, and I can't go myself. It seems very strange since Annie's da and mam must surely be at home."

"Not a'tall. I'll go right away. Maybe her mother is taken with something and Annie doesn't know what to do. If that's the case, I'll get my mother. I know there is not a lot of money to spare, and they would not want to send for the doctor." As good as her word, she darted out and ran to the end of the lane where the McVeigh cottage was located.

As she walked to the door it opened, and Mrs. McVeigh came out. She was untidy, with wisps of hair pulling out of the bun on the nape of her neck as she twisted and pleated her apron about her callused, rough hands. Her eyes were red and her face haggard from lack of sleep. Mary was shocked; this was not like the woman. Annie's mam, like Ellen, always strove to be neat and tidy. Mary was alarmed.

"Oh Mary," she cried. "Maybe you can do something with her. Himself and I have been up all night and she won't say a word. He's gone off to do a day's work with neither sleep nor tea, but we're afraid to leave her alone."

"Mrs. McVeigh, I don't know what you're telling me. Is something wrong with Annie? I saw her only yesterday at the factory. She was all right then."

"Oh Mary, Mary dear, you haven't heard." And with that the tears started to roll down her face.

"Annie only heard last night. Aemon's brother came to tell her that the telegram had come. He's dead, he's dead. And my poor Annie just sits there. She hasn't moved from the spot she was in when the lad blurted out the news. Go into her, Mary. See if you can help her. She just stares at her da and me and we can't get her to say a word. Go ahead, Mary. I'll make a pot of tea."

Mary stood speechless and terrified as Mrs. McVeigh hurried off to put the kettle on the hob. Reluctantly she entered the house and was directed by a nod from Mrs. McVeigh to a dark corner of the kitchen where Annie was sitting, huddled into herself, staring with dilated eyes into some unfathomable deep.

Mary approached slowly so that Annie would be aware of her presence, but it would not have mattered. She did not appear to see anything. Desperately Mary tried to think of what her mother would do. She began to chafe Annie's cold fingers and remembered that her mother always built up fire for comfort and warmth when things were going badly. She looked about for peat, which her mother piled lavishly at home, but she saw no supply by the hearth and realized it would be an embarrassment to ask. Clearly there was not the abundance here to which she was accustomed at home.

She stood thinking for awhile and then half lifted, half dragged Annie to a chair near the hearth where the kettle was steaming and wrapped her in a shawl thrown over an old rocker placed near the small fire. She took the hot tea from the mother and asked for sugar. This too was a luxury, but Mrs. McVeigh produced a small bit in a bowl. Vowing to replace the sugar as soon as possible, Mary spooned a large amount into the cup and topped it off with the cream from the little pitcher. Mary whispered to Mrs. McVeigh that she would stay with Annie if she would like to lie down for a bit. Gratefully the woman accepted the offer and took herself into the room off the kitchen.

Mary, with the tea in her hand, knelt on a little stool in front of Annie and, alternately crooning and chiding, repeated a litany, "Annie, Annie asthore, drink a little of this now, dear. This is Mary. Come now Annie, drink up, sweeting. There's a good girl. Isn't that good now. Have a little more."

Finally the tea was drunk and some warmth appeared in Annie's face. Mary put the teacup down and, propping herself on the arm of the chair, pulled Annie's head to her breast and rocked her. After a bit Annie lifted her face to Mary and said, "I'll never be safe again. Never, never."

"Oh Annie achree, why would you say that? Don't you have a family and friends who love you? Aren't you a young girl with a life to live?"

"Mary, Mary, you don't understand. Nobody does. Aemon was my mother, my father — the only person I needed in the whole world. I was safe with him, Mary. He took care of me. And he would have all my life if they hadn't killed him." With that she burst into sobs, but Mary was grateful for this, as she remembered too well the dark silence from her mother last year. She thought the tears were better.

"Mary?"

"Yes, Annie love, what is it?"

"God is punishing me."

The tears rushed into Mary's eyes. She had never known a sweeter, more gentle girl. Holding the weeping girl closer to herself she said, "God is not punishing you, Annie. Many people have lost boys in this war. Why do you say that."

"I loved Aemon better that anyone. Better than my God. The only thing I could ever think of when I should have been at my prayers in church was how handsome Aemon was with the colors from the windows flickering on his hair. I truly never cared what happened to anyone as long as I had Aemon."

"Annie, listen to me. Sure you're just a young lass who loved a boy she'd known all her life. God made you. Do you think He did not understand you? Put it out of your mind, asthore. I promise you God is not punishing you."

The dialogue continued intermittently for hours. "Mary, I loved him too well ... Mary, I'll never be safe again."

"Ah, not a'tall, Annie. Aren't you the lovely girl and won't there be another one day."

"No Mary, never. I'll never be safe again."

Mary held Annie, rocking her and assuring her that her life was not over. At last, from sheer exhaustion, Annie fell asleep. By this time Annie's mother had taken a little rest and tidied herself. Between the two of them they managed to tuck Annie into her bed. By then Mary wanted nothing more than to be home with her own mother.

The news had gotten to Leiter before Mary. Ellen had the tea ready and sat with Mary by the fire to hear what she had to say. Mary was very distraught. Annie's reaction to Aemon's death was strange.

"It's almost as if she were grieving for her own death or life or something. I didn't know what to say to her except the same things over and over again."

"Mary dear, just being there and holding her was the best you could do. I'm afraid, asthore, that there is little comfort for her, and we must pray she recovers from this.

"Her mother has always been worried about Annie. She is not like the younger ones. Since Annie was very little she has been fearful. Mrs. McVeigh was always grateful for Aemon. Annie seemed happy when he was about, and her mother thought she was getting past the fearful, high-strung way she has. God knows what will happen now.

"You did your best, Mary. Go into your bed, child, your eyes are like two burned holes in a blanket."

Ellen sat a long time by the fire after Mary went to bed. Finally, shaking her head at the futility of war and despairing of Annie's future, she tidied and went to her own.

The war limped and dragged on. Blood-drenched reports from the front horrified everyone but left those with immediate concern numb with terror and fear. Despite America's participation, there seemed to be no relief from the insane slaughter.

The church was full at every service, and prayers rose

with every puff of incense for the safety of loved ones. Mary, who was often on her knees praying for the schismatic boy she loved, wondered how God kept His sanity. Did not the mother of a young German soldier have as much right to pray for him as any Irish woman intent on telling her beads for the safety of her son? For that matter, did God recognize the prayers of an Irish girl for the hated sassenach? Knowing there was no answer to these questions, even if she were foolhardy enough to ask them, she continued to pray, hoping that God knew what He was doing.

Between worry about Leslie, guilt that she had not yet spoken to her mother about him, and concern for Annie, Mary's days were harassed and busy.

Mary asked her mother, "Don't you think Annie should be coming around a bit by now? She comes to the factory but does not really seem to be there. I've been after her to come with me to the dances, but she just shakes her head. Annie loved to dance."

"Well, Mary, it's hard to say. Annie had all her eggs in the one basket. She thought her life began and ended with Aemon. Everything she did was with the one thought in mind: That he would marry her and take care of her the rest of her life. It's not like that — everyone has to turn their own wheel, and I'm afraid poor Annie doesn't even know where hers is right now. The only thing to do, child dear, is wait and see. It's up to Annie herself to do the trick. We can only wait to help her if she needs it."

Ellen had no more to say despite Mary's efforts to prolong the discussion. Privately Ellen thought the girl would never recover. It wasn't just that she had lost Aemon. She seemed to be missing the will to live. Ellen thought of all the old tales about the wee people stealing the spirits of young people. She shook herself. It wouldn't do for Mary to think there was no hope. Mary herself was the best medicine Annie could hope for, and it wouldn't do to have the cure overcome by the disease.

To change the subject, Ellen said, "I saw Annie's grandda in the town today. He was coming along at a great pace with his three-legged gait. I only waved to him from the shop, for I knew he was on his way to his pint and card game. As he passed I saw two riders, an Englishman and his lady, coming along the main street. I didn't recognize them — they must be visitors to the garrison. When they came to old McVeigh, the Englishman hit him on the shoulder with his crop. It startled the poor soul since he hadn't even seen the riders coming – his mind was elsewhere."

And Ellen shared the rest:

The Englishman said, "You there, we seem to be lost."

McVeigh looked at him and said, "Sure, not a'tall. You're never lost. Aren't you there in front of me on the main street? Divil a'lost you are. Good day to you then."

He tipped his hat and started down the street.

The Englishman was furious, and the lady looked as if she'd swallowed something bad. The man turned and rode up to McVeigh again. This time the horse was almost on top of the old man.

"Listen, you ignorant savage, I need directions. Do you understand? How do we return to the garrison?"

"Oh begods, your lordship, I didn't take your meaning. I'll be happy to give you directions."

"Well, Mary," Ellen said to her daughter, "that Englishman got his directions, but it would be a wonder if they ever saw the garrison before nightfall. McVeigh gave the best and clearest directions I ever heard, but they led across every bog and pit in the township. The old man is a marvel. Sharp as a tack."

"Won't the English try to find the old man and punish him?" asked Mary.

"Och, they have better things to do right now than search out Mr. McVeigh. Besides, the Englishman may be too embarrassed to admit he was made a fool by an old man. When the riders were out of sight, he waved his cane after them and went on his way singing that I.R.A. song 'God Help This Country'."

# IX

The summer was over, and the days were closing in. The hay was gathered, the peat was cut, and everyone waited for news of the end of the war. Mary was free from the factory for a few days while they prepared a special order.

One morning, to her delight and surprise, she saw Leslie's ship at anchor. In her eagerness to finish the chores Ellen had asked her to do, she aroused her mother's suspicions.

"You are in a fair mood this day. What is it that is making you so cheerful? You have certainly been down in the mouth for a good while now. Is there something you are not telling me?" asked Ellen.

"Why do you ask such a thing? I'm just pleased to be away from the factory for a few days. I was thinking, mother, I would like to stop by Mrs. Blaine's and ask her to make up a new frock for me." Expecting a homily on throwing money around as if it were water, Mary added anxiously, "My old party gown is loose, and it would need to be altered anyway. I have some money put away. I won't spend too much."

Ellen's heart wrenched at the anxiety in Mary's face. "Well indeed," she thought to herself, "does the child think I am so terrible that I have no memory of being young and wanting a new frock?"

Aloud she said, "And sure it is no wonder you're in need

of a new dress. You could be pulled through the eye of a big needle, you're that thin. Stop at Catherine's, but tell her I'll be by to arrange a trade for it. Keep your money, child dear. You deserve something pretty. Now go and enjoy yourself — you also deserve a little pleasure. I'll see you for tea."

As soon as she finished the last of the tasks, Mary scrubbed and put on the neatest of her skirts and middies. Trying to look casual she waved to her mother saying, "I'm off. I'll be back for tea with all the news from the village."

Secretly she hugged to herself the thought that she would certainly have news when she returned. When she had last seen Leslie he was full of information about Canada and Australia. Two of the men on the ship had spent some years there and were "a veritable mine of information," according to Leslie. He said that based on their information and what he could read in the material available, he would make a decision about their destination.

Although the thought of leaving her home and her mother was dreadful, the prospect of new lands and being with Leslie overcame all her fears.

Mary had made the trip to Fintra many times, but today it seemed she would never reach her destination. Finally, to her joy, she rounded the bend and started down the little path to the strand. She proceeded carefully, for if Leslie was ahead of her and heard her coming, he was in the habit of surprising her. When she got clear of the trees, she saw that he was there ahead of her. But something was not right.

Leslie, in full uniform, stood staring out at the water, hands clasped behind his back. As he heard the skittering of the rocky shale, he turned to look at her. Withdrawn and white-faced, he held out his hands to her. She clasped them and in a shaking voice said, "What is it?"

"My brother is dead. He was killed in the attack at Villeret." With a catch in his voice he continued, "We are so near the end. Why did this have to happen?"

Mary reached for him. Putting her arms about him, she patted his shoulders. She had not yet absorbed all the effects of his brother's death, but she knew her dreams were done.

"I'm on emergency leave and must go very soon. I could not leave without seeing you. My father has taken very ill. He was working long hours without proper food and rest, and my mother said the news almost killed him. They want me home, and I must go. My brother was trained since a baby to care for the estate and all the people on it. Now there is no one but me. Mary ... Mary?"

"I know what you are saying. You cannot emigrate, and I certainly can't go with you to your parents. There is nothing to be done," Mary said.

"Oh Mary, I did not and would not ever choose the life they are thrusting at me. When I was little I always felt sorry for my brother, who had to be tip-top at everything and always on display. My dream was a life of my own, away from all the protocol and tradition. Now look at me. Tied into it like a Christmas goose. Mary, how will I live without you? Is there any way?"

Shaking her head, Mary replied, "You know as well as I, Leslie, that I would never be accepted in your world. Even if there weren't the question of religion, I don't have the polish or training to be the mistress of a great estate. It might be lovely for awhile – being together – but sooner or later we would both be miserable. It's better to end it now."

With that she pulled back from him, trying desperately

not to let the tears flow.

Leslie took her hands once more and said, "I must tell you, Mary, that I will marry. The estate requires more than I can do by myself. My mother was always busy and I will need the same kind of help. But this I swear to you, Mary, no one will ever take your place in my heart. You were the girl I dreamed of when I planned my life."

"Who will you marry, Leslie? Some beautiful English lady who knows how to curtsy to the Queen?", this said with some bitterness.

"Ah, Mary, I have had time to think of my future since I received the wireless. I expect I will be urged to marry Elizabeth, the girl who was affianced to my brother. They were friends from childhood and always expected to marry. She is some years older than I and she knows more about the land than I do. Her father's lands are adjacent to ours, and she was raised to be the mistress of an estate. It will not be a love match, Mary. When you see the announcement in the *Times*, remember that my heart is lost to you.

"Elizabeth does not love me, but we will manage. Her love and hopes, I am sure, were with my brother. They waited for the war to be over. My brother would not marry for fear of coming home damaged. If they had married, she might have had a child by now.

"Now she has nothing — we will be a well matched pair.

"I wish I could stay longer with you — or maybe I don't. Nothing will make this easy."

He reached for her. Pulling her as tightly to himself as possible, he held her for a long time. Tears were running down his face when he finally released her with quick kisses on her eyelids. Turning, he ran away from the strand.

Watching him until he turned a bend and could no longer be seen, Mary stood pushing her nails into the palms of her hands until, looking down, she realized she was in pain. Her tears started to flow. Not the hot, stormy torrents of a small child but quiet, despairing tears – the overflow of a broken heart.

Without thinking she sat on the rock they had often shared on warm summer days. When she realized this, she jumped up. She knew she would never see him again or share any news or laughter with him. With a hysterical sob she wondered who would want to hear all the funny things Michael Og did now that Leslie was gone.

When Mary arrived at Leiter, cold, drained and exhausted, tea was over. Her brother was gone off to finish the evening chores, and her sisters Lena and Sally were squabbling about their turns to clean up. With her back to the door Ellen was mopping Michael who had been, as usual, very enthusiastic with his tea.

In a scolding voice she said over her shoulder, "And do you think tea is served at all hours, my girl? You will have to help yourself."

As she said this Ellen turned to add further weight to her displeasure. She looked at the pale, staring girl who had been so bright and cheerful in the morning, and her heart felt as if it had stopped.

"Girls, girls, stop your quarreling. Out with you. Out to the barn and give your brother a hand. God knows he could use a little help. Take Michael with you but by all the saints don't let him out of your sight. Out with you."

Ellen walked to where Mary stood, seemingly unable to move. She took Mary's hand and brought her to the fire.

After removing Mary's wet shoes and placing a cup of strong tea in her hands, she sat and waited for Mary to speak.

When the tea had warmed her insides and the fire had taken the cold from her bones, some color came back to Mary's face. Ellen was sitting quietly with the workbox in her lap – waiting, Mary knew, for an explanation.

Ellen was indeed waiting. Mary did not appear to have suffered any injury. She was not ill. And to the best of Ellen's knowledge, Mary had no involvement with any of the young lads from the village. Although she knew her daughter loved to dance and went anywhere there was a promise of music and fun, she had not, as far as Ellen knew, formed any attachment. If she wasn't upset about a young man, Ellen couldn't for the life of her think why Mary was so unhinged. Any news of trouble in Killybegs would have reached Ellen by now. She waited.

When Mary, between sobs and tears, began to tell her mother about Leslie, Ellen dropped her hands into her lap and held her breath. The words "English" and "midshipman" sent a wave of terror through her. She listened quietly, but as the story evolved she began to relax a little. It did not appear her worst fears were to be confirmed.

If Mary had become pregnant and abandoned, the consequences in any case would have been severe. In this small community, general knowledge that the clandestine father was an Englishman would have been almost unbearable. Any girl finding herself in that unfortunate condition would be shunned, and her family would share the punishment. It would then be years before Lena and Sally, particularly, would be able to enter into village life.

When Mary finished her story, Ellen carefully

questioned her, but Mary's obvious puzzlement caused her to abandon that inquiry and focus on Mary's sorrow.

"Mother, I know I should have told you about Leslie sooner, but at first he was just a friend to talk to, and I never thought of anything else. But every time he came back from sea, he seemed to need my company more and more. At first I was sorry for him — no one seemed to write to him or send packages — but then I started to care for him. We realized we both felt the same way the last time he was in port. He was making plans for us, and he did want to come to speak with you, but I asked him to wait until he had worked out his intentions and until I told you about him. Now it doesn't matter anymore and I'll never see him again." With that she burst into tears again.

Ellen sighed and wished once again that George were here to help. Mary and her father had shared a relationship that did not exist between Ellen and her eldest daughter. Never having experienced it, Ellen could not share or understand the wild streak that seemed to be the core of Mary's being. George on the other hand seemed to be able to talk to her and counsel her. Well, thought Ellen, I can try.

"Listen to me, child dear. You have the comfort of knowing that he cared for you. If things had been different, both of you could have emigrated and made a life away from all this hatred. But Mary, he was raised to be what he is and to his credit he would not, could not turn away from his background when his parents needed him.

"He himself said it is not the life he would choose, and by his own admission he can foresee what it will be like when he puts his shoulder to the wheel. He will look back all his life, Mary, and ask himself what might have been.

"Some of your tears should be for him. You don't believe me now, but your sorrow will ease. You're young and have a life to look forward to."

Ellen put her arms around her daughter and, swallowing the tears that threatened to spill out said, "I wish with all of my heart that you did not have all this sadness. But if wishes had wings, I could fly. So dry your tears one more time, my good girl, and we'll have another cup of tea. Maybe we could get a few people in for a wee dance before the winter sets in. Would you like that?"

§ § §

Since there was no cure but time for the lovesickness that ailed Mary, she threw herself into every event that was brought to her attention. She had always been popular because of her readiness to join in any scheme, but now her activities were almost feverish. If there were horse races along the strand, or a party of young people attempting to climb the forbidding cliffs looming over the Atlantic, or dancing through the night, Mary was there. Ellen watched but knew there was little she could do until the frenzy exhausted itself.

Parties and dances were many that winter – some in honor of the safe return of a son, some in farewell to a son or daughter off to seek fortune in a gentler land. At one of the farewell parties Mary was asked to dance by Alphonsus, a young man who had been friends with her brother Michael. They whirled and stepped through a prolonged eight-hand reel then, breathless and thirsty, went looking for something in the way of refreshment. They found gallons of tea ready for the asking, and with cups in hand went looking for a spot to sit and catch their breath.

As they passed the door Alphonsus's tea was well laced, courtesy of the men standing in a group by the door. "Ah, lads," he said, "many a time in the trenches I would have given my soul and all for a drop of the creature. I thank you." Then Mary and he proceeded into the yard and found a spot to sit by the side of the cottage.

They sat quietly sipping for awhile, watching the young ones dancing in the yard. Alphonsus became pensive, staring into his cup and swirling the liquid around and around. Finally he said, "Mary, I'm sorry I have not been up to see your mother since I returned from France. I heard about Michael, Paddy and John. Her heart must be broken, and then to lose your father also. I'm sorry, Mary."

"Thank you, Alphonsus. We've come a ways since then. I think sometimes my mother is so busy she doesn't have a chance to grieve. I do hear her at night sometimes crying and going around her rosary, and then I know she can't sleep thinking about all of them. I wish there was something I could do, but I can't think what it would be. I suppose you heard that she took Michael Og from his mother. He's been a comfort to her. He's helped all of us. He's very taking.

"But I have to say my mother did wonder that you didn't come to visit her. She thought you were busy making the rounds and getting back into a routine – but by now you should have found time to sit and have a chat. She remembers how close you were with Michael. She'll be glad to see you when you have the chance," Mary replied.

"Arrah, Mary, it was not for lack of time. It was pure cowardice. I know she will ask me questions about what life was like for us in the trenches, and I don't know how I can lie without giving myself away. If I said to you it was pure hell, Mary, you still would not see how bad it was. It wasn't only the mud, the smells, the belly cramps, the filth of the privies, the rats, the poor food, the constant noise and lack of sleep. The worst of it was the screams of some poor bastard with his belly ripped open lying under the German guns. Ofttimes I wanted to shoot to put the poor sod out of his misery, but even when I could bring myself to do it, the range was too far. When I heard Michael was dead, I would lie and wonder how he died. Did ye ever hear?" Alphonsus asked.

"No," Mary replied. "All we received was a telegram saying he was missing and presumed dead."

"Ah well, sometimes it's best not to know everything. That's why I'm afraid to face your mother, Mary. She could always read me like a book, and she would have the whole story out of me.

"But as bad as the trenches were, even the English had to put up with those conditions, excepting the staff officers behind the lines. And sure to what purpose? They will be at it again as soon as they catch their breath. To add insult to injury, the Irish were treated like the slops you would throw to the pigs. Irish recruits were just so much gun fodder, pushed into the trenches with hardly any training and out again into no man's land when the officers felt they could gain an inch of ground. It was a slaughter, Mary. Fifty-thousand Irishman in a war that was not of their making for a country that despises them. The wonder is not how many died but the miracle that any of us survived at all.

"No matter what they say, the English will never treat us as equals. Their own class system places commoners way below the salt. How can we expect any fairness when they consider us a conquered people to be used as they see fit?"

"What will you do? Will you stay in Ireland?"

"I have no one to hold me here. The old ones are dead and my brother has the farm. I'm more than welcome to stay, but that can only be for awhile. He'll be getting married. I don't know. I've thought of America, but then I think I'll be wasting all the military training I've gotten by order of the crown. There are those who say my talents could be put to use here. Since there is no one who cares except my brother, it would be nice to be wanted."

"Don't say that. I hate to hear of anyone joining the cause ever since Paddy and...."

Choked up with tears, Mary couldn't complete her thought. But Alphonsus answered.

"Ah, but Mary, this time we have the advantage of some training from the enemy, and I hear there will be money from America to help us along. Sure aren't your own uncles helping to raise money for the cause? No, no, Mary, this time the English won't be dealing with young dreamers having more hope than help. There is a core of trained soldiers. And if there are enough, I think we can get the English foot off our neck this time."

"Alphonsus, don't you want to marry and make a life for yourself? If you go on the run, you know how hard it is to escape from that life. Haven't you had enough of fighting? There must be a girl you would want to marry."

"I'm not much in the marrying line, Mary. Never cared for the girls. If your brother had stayed away from the one he got caught up with, he'd be alive today. But Michael was different than me; he was always the man for a pretty face.

"No. I think I'll take my talents to Dublin and see who I

can join up with. Of course," he said with a grin, holding his teacup high, "it will mean giving up some of the pleasures of life. But isn't that the way of things?

"But you, Mary, what about you? There is nothing in this country for a beautiful, smart young woman. Get out of this country, Mary, things will be worse before they get better. Go to your brother, Eddie. He will be back from the American army by now and he will help you. I mean it Mary. Chance it. Go."

Then, hurling the dregs of his cup to the ground, he rose and pulling her by the hand said, "Och, enough maudling, Mary, come away. We'll have another wee dance for Michael. How he did love to dance."

Shortly after that Alphonsus left without any farewells. There was no further word from him, but the conversation continued to nag at Mary.

# X

Throughout the winter, Ellen had been watching Mary. She ached for her daughter but knew there was little to do but wait. She also felt in her heart that Mary would not stay with her. There was, God knows, little future for the young people in Ireland. And despite all her frantic efforts to forget Leslie, Mary had not come upon any young man who could supplant him in her affections.

Ellen sighed. She knew she would watch from the hilltop while another child journeyed to America.

Mary herself had no idea what was troubling her. She told herself, over and over again, that she no longer pined for Leslie. She had seen the announcement of his coming marriage in the *London Times*. Her mother still took the paper, as her father had done for so many years. The item in the paper confirmed what Leslie had said. He was to marry the girl who had been affianced to his brother. The paper hailed it as a union of two fine old families. That was that, she told herself.

She also told herself that she was well done for with a good home, a job that took care of any little luxuries she might want, many friends and grand parties. What then was the matter? And then after the lecture to herself she would be caught unawares. Sometimes in the gray, early morning or in the long, mauve twilight she would stand gazing out to sea, and the silhouette of one of Leslie's fleet would heave over the horizon, skimming along on the tide, bound for the calm and comfort of the harbor. Unbidden, the tears would flow, but they did little to wash away the pain in her heart.

It was in this mood that Mary went one beautiful summer evening to a gathering in the next town. She had finally persuaded Annie to come with her, and she was glad of it. Everyone was fussing and making much of Annie. They were pleased to see her out and about once again. The music and dancing were in full swing and Annie was being kindly passed from partner to partner when Mary, with a cup of tea in her hand, slipped away into the yard.

As the musicians sounded the bars of the next dance, Mary could hear her name called to join the next set, but she wanted to sit with her thoughts. In the gloaming, the hills and surrounding countryside shimmered and slid from shadow to pale luminescence. The air was heavy with the smell of ripening hay and the heart-rending scent of roses. With an ache in her heart that she dare not name, Mary sat sipping her tea, and as her eyes adjusted to the dimness, she began to heed the little dramas taking place around her.

Away in the darkest corner a bunch of the young lads puffed furiously at their gaspers and listened intently to the man in their midst. She did not know him, but she knew his business and she wanted to shout, "No more, no more. Aren't there enough dead already," but she knew she wouldn't say it, and they wouldn't listen if she did. The young men were convinced that now was the time to strike for liberty and freedom, and those who would gainsay were brushed aside – as it had always been and would always be.

Some of the young crowd, pushed into the yard for lack of space in the house, were dancing and laughing at a distance from the recruiter and his disciples. They made her feel very old.

In the shadow of the barn, a little distance from the dancers, she saw a tall young man leaning in a manner that prevented the giggling girl, with her back pressed against the barn wall, from escaping. Mary smiled slightly in recognition of the first moves of courtship. Then, startled, she realized that the lad she was looking at was her younger brother. She drew in her breath, and shaking her head she acknowledged that he was now probably of a marrying age. A little young perhaps, but with the responsibility of the farm on his shoulders it would be hard to deny him the right to marry.

And then what would her position be? The unmarried oldest daughter living at home with her mother, two young sisters, a brother, a young sister-in-law and nephew. She bent her head and began to cry, letting the tears slip into the cup she was still holding.

After a bit she dried her eyes. Sitting up straight she looked long and lovingly at the beauty of the countryside. She breathed in the perfume of the summer night and then rose with her decision made. There was no help for it – she must emigrate or stagnate.

On the way home she told her friend Annie what she had decided. For a long time there was silence, and then with a trembling voice Annie said, "I will go to America with you. My auntie, my mother's sister, has written a few times to say she could find a good place for me in Boston. While you were here I would not go, but after you leave there will be no one for me, and I might as well be in America. My mam and da don't know what to do about me, and God knows they have a houseful of young ones to worry about. They think it would be an opportunity for me. I'll go."

"Annie, Annie, listen to me. America is a big place. I am not sure where this Boston is, and I don't know where I will be. My brother will help me, but he is in Bridgeport, wherever that is. Think on it awhile before you decide."

"No. I've decided. It's no use to talk Mary. I don't belong at home and I probably don't belong in America, but I don't care anymore and that's the truth of it."

Recognizing that her persuasion was useless, and hoping that Annie's parents would see the folly of sending their gentle daughter so far from all she knew, Mary said no more.

The following morning, determined not to lose her resolve, Mary told her mother what she had decided. Ellen knew there was no point in arguing. Nor would she. Better than her daughter she knew the dreary prospect for a young woman with no place of her own.

Once again Ellen kept her heartbreak to herself and helped Mary to make arrangements. Letters and telegrams flew across the Atlantic.

Fortunately, Mary's brother Eddie was eager to show off the prosperity he had experienced in America. After serving in the American army, Eddie had returned to Bridgeport to his uncles and cousins. The McGuinness uncles had prospered in the steel mills as labor leaders and in their connections with the Democratic party, which welcomed the immigrant Irish and turned a blind eye to any accusation of fund-raising for Irish causes. Their sons and daughters were American and had, at the insistence of their parents, become lawyers and teachers. As shrewd as they were daring, the McGuinness brothers had been quick to recognize where the power base lay.

Because of his exceptional war record and their connections, they were able to place Eddie in a good position in the city. He arranged for Mary's passage and wrote to say he would meet her ship. The accommodations he arranged were superior to what Mary had planned for herself. Ellen was very grateful for this, since Mary's excitement at the prospect of such luxury helped her through the months of waiting.

Although Annie had hopes of sailing to America with Mary, it was not to be. The family for whom Annie was engaged to work had advanced the money for her passage in steerage. Mary did not plan to leave until the harvest was in and the peat cut – then her mother and brother would be able to manage for the winter. Annie's aunt did not have patience to wait for Mary, and Mrs. McVeigh was anxious that Annie might lose a good opportunity. Weeping and pale, Annie came to say goodbye to Mary.

"I wish I were going with you. It might be that I could learn to live without Aemon. You have been a good friend, Mary. I hope we meet again."

Mary put her arms around Annie. "Don't speak like that. We will meet again in America. Remember how young and pretty you are. America will be a fine chance for a new life."

As Mary watched her go down the hillside, she wished once again that Annie's parents would reconsider what they were doing to the shy, timid girl, but she knew they had a flock of young McVeighs to raise and not much to share among them. She sighed and entered the house.

As soon as it was known that Mary intended to emigrate, she was awash in requests from people with relatives in the states to carry a little something to them, to contact one who was remiss in their correspondence, or to visit an ailing relative. Unaware of the vast distances between all these points, Mary agreed to all except ungainly packages. She was to regret her kindness for a year and more.

Catherine Blaine came one evening with a beautifully tailored traveling suit. Mary was speechless with pleasure. And in response to Ellen's protestations Catherine merely replied, "Well Ellen, my dear, I could do no less. In all these years you and I have helped each other. And I know how sorely you will miss Mary, but we could not have her arriving in America looking like something the cat dragged in on a wet night. She will look lovely, and that will help her in the strangeness of a new country. Besides that, she hasn't seen her brother Eddie or my son Patrick in years. I think they will be surprised."

With all that had to be done, the time passed quickly. The night before Mary was to leave for Cobh, people came from near and far for the American wake. Ellen had outdone herself in the kitchen, aided and abetted by her sister-in-law Tessa. Both women were heartsore, knowing how much they would miss Mary. She had contributed in no small measure to the social life of Killybegs and was known for her willingness to help in any emergency.

In direct proportion to the grief over her departure, the party escalated into a most memorable occasion. The gaiety and size of the wake was a tribute to both Mary and Ellen.

Early in the morning with the party still roaring on, Mary slipped upstairs to gather the last few things she would carry with her. Her trunk was already loaded on the cart for the trip to the railroad. She stood in the bedroom she had shared all these years with her sisters and wondered how she ever decided to go to America. She knew it was too late to change anything, but tired and overwrought, she wished there were some other road for her to take. She looked at her bed and saw Michael Og rolled into a ball with his thumb in his mouth.

Many a night she had been awakened from sleep by his soft, whispered, "Maimie, Maimie, I frightened." Reaching out for the wee one, she would nestle his little body against hers and they would drift to sleep in the security of warmth and love. And now, too young to comprehend the finality of her departure, he was aware only that his Maimie was going away, and he had been very unhappy for days.

Mary bent over him and as she kissed his damp, tearstained face, her own tears started, and she whirled quickly away lest she awaken him. She could not bear to hold him and have him taken from her arms.

Running downstairs, she entered the kitchen with her coat and traveling bag in her hands. Ellen caught sight of her and went to her side. Mary's brother had already taken possession of the coat and bag and was standing in the yard by the wagon with Tessa's son, who would return with the cart after seeing them onto the train. Mary's brother would further accompany her to Cobh.

All in the kitchen gathered to kiss, hug or shake her hand, wish her luck and God-speed. Her mother walked with her to the cart. No one interrupted, and they stood looking at each other, unable to say what was in their hearts.

Finally, Ellen reached for Mary and drew her head to her

breast saying, "God bless you and keep you and may he hold his hand over you all the days of your life, child dear. I know you have to leave, and I will miss you, but work hard and write often. Remember there is always a home for you if things don't go well for you in America."

Ellen released her, and Mary climbed into the cart. The pain in her chest was so severe she could hardly breath. The cart started down the road, but she did not look back — besides, she knew her mother would not watch the cart disappear around the bend in the road.

The trip to Cobh was long and dreary. The seats in the train offered little in the way of comfort, but Mary and her brother, exhausted from lack of sleep, dozed intermittently all the way to the south. When they were awake they stared fascinated at the changing landscape. Neither had been further than thirty or so miles from their home — until now. Accustomed to the harsh, wild hills and stretches of uninhabited land in the north, the gentle, fertile midlands were a revelation to them.

Finally the train arrived at Cobh. Anxious and tired, they found the pier where Mary would board the tender to the ship waiting in the harbor. Most passengers had boarded in Southampton; the ship would sail on the next tide.

Overcome by her conflicting emotions, Mary could only hug her brother and bid him a safe journey home. He was struggling with the sorrow of parting and the need to appear to be the man he was endeavoring to be. As the tender pulled away from the pier, he brushed the traitor tears from his eyes and turned abruptly away.

Mary found a seat hidden in a corner and let the tears flow down her cheeks. She had no choice — they would come no matter what. She remained there, grateful for the privacy, until the tender positioned itself next to the liner and she and her luggage were transferred aboard.

A steward recognized the rawness of grief and lack of sophistication. He took pity on the lovely girl, guided her to her cabin, and introduced her to the young woman who would share the cabin with her. He advised them that the dinner bell would ring shortly, and he left them.

Mary's roommate would not go to the dining room. She had been crying since she left her home and lay on her bunk exhausted, saying she would not move 'til morning. Mary had not eaten all day, and if truth were known had not really had a meal in several days. She went to the dining room hoping for a good cup of tea.

There were few in the dining room. Those who came were not inclined to conversation, and the waiters stood at their stations prepared to serve quarts of tea with the bread and rolls on the table. They knew that other food would be ignored. They had seen immigrants many times and were bored. Mary tried to force some of the proffered dinner down but gave up quickly and gratefully accepted the hot tea, for it was a remembrance of home and comfort.

After dinner the great shipped lurched and the throbbing of the engines could be felt as it prepared to leave the harbor. Mary went up on deck. The bow of the ship was already turned to the west, but Mary went to the stern to watch the coastline of Ireland. Night was gathering very rapidly, and as the ship rounded the Head of Kinsale it turned pitch black, and she could no longer see land.

But then, on the southernmost tip of land at the highest point, a flicker of flame could be seen, and it burst into a blazing beam of fire. On each hill running up the Irish coast, the fires were lit; bonfires stretched as far as could be seen.

Mary had forgotten that tonight was Halloween, the eve of All Souls Day. The watch fires would burn until morning. She had thought there were no more tears left in her, but at the memory of the many times she had danced and sung around the watch fires, sorrow welled up once more until, drained and tired, she looked again and saw only darkness.

The ship, safely away from shore, had picked up speed. Mary left the darkness of the stern and walked to the bow. She heard music. First-class passengers were being regaled with the latest music from New York and London. Softly, as if an accompaniment to the dance tunes, the sounds of tinkling glassware and murmured conversation drifted into the chill night air. From the other passengers, all that could be heard was the mournful music of the displaced: songs of home and sadness.

Listening, she stood at the bow and watched the spume reflect the light from the sleek, towering ship as it sped, plunging and heaving, toward America, where she would find her brother ... and Patrick.

FINIS

# Notes on the Author

Evelyn Blaine Durkin, daughter to Mary Meehan Blaine and Patrick George Blaine, was born in Washington Heights NYC in 1931. In May 1932 she returned to her parents' hometown Killybegs, County Donegal via ship with her mother and elder sister Myra Blaine Ruocco as Mary carried unborn Patrick George. The family disembarked via tender into the shallow waters of Belfast Harbor, Mary toting Evelyn while holding Myra's hand as they waded to shore. Finding little solace in Killybegs from The Depression, they embarked again for New York a year later.

Dede, as Evelyn came to be called, grew up in The Heights with her parents, sister and brother in a household deemed the first stop in New York City for Donegal émigrés then seeking a foothold in America. Blaine-Meehan céilís continued through their childhood, anchored by a pair of stand-up pianos parked back-to-back in Pop & Mary's center room and a beer keg in the bathroom tub.

DeDe attended Hunter College, married the young Korean War veteran Francis "Buddy" Durkin in 1953, and in 1960 left Washington Heights for Ossining, NY, raising Laura, Claire, Mark and Jenifer.

In 1985 DeDe and Bud moved to Long Beach, NY. In 1988 they celebrated the birth of their first granddaughter Marisa Blaine Zipay, with Marisa's parents Laura & Steve living nearby. There they also enjoyed the births and growth of five additional grandchildren: Claire & Rich's Bridget & Cara Fasciani, Nanette Mueller & Mark Durkin's Belle Durkin, and Jenifer Durkin & Benjamin Levy's Nathaniel & Declan Levy.

# Notes on the Author (cont'd)

In her forties, DeDe began her career in reinsurance, which took her to Mission Re and AmRe Brokers. On 9/11, still consulting at the age of 70, DeDe was working on Fulton Street in NYC, across Broadway from the twin towers. She employed her ample New York moxie to escape north via taxi. She returned to work less than two weeks later, haunted by "the pall" hanging over the area.

After Bud passed in 1998, DeDe lived on Manhattan's Upper West Side, not far from her childhood home, until her death in 2011.

Daughters of Donegal *is published posthumously by the author's children. May DeDe's grandchildren, nieces, nephews and extended family enjoy the stories.*

Evelyn "DeDe" Durkin, 2006

Made in the USA
Middletown, DE
03 October 2022

11607938R00142